# CALL TO THE HUNT

*Moonlight glints through the trees, pulling at your heart. Your skin feels alive, flowing. The pain is incredible, unimaginable—bones shattering and reshaping. You pass out for a moment, awake to a rush of new sensations, new scents. The trees call to run, the air calls for blood, the moon calls to the hunt....*

**Werewolf Saga** author Steven E. Wedel brings you a collection of 12 lycanthropic legends including:

- Journey to a New World
- Of Witches and Werewolves
- The Feast of Saratoga
- Elysia
- Call to the Hunt
- Latent Lycanthropy
- Biological Clock
- Show Me
- Sunday Dentistry
- Kiss of the Wolf
- To Be A Mother

The Scrybe Press edition features an introduction by noted genre author *Kelley Armstrong* and contains four stories not in the original MoonHowler Press edition, three of which are previously unpublished.

# CALL TO THE HUNT

STEVEN E. WEDEL

WITH AN INTRODUCTION BY
KELLEY ARMSTRONG

# SCRYBE PRESS

This is a work of fiction. All the characters and events portrayed in this novel are either fictitious or are used fictitiously.

A Scrybe Press Publication
Published by Scrybe Press
Massena, NY 13662

www.scrybepress.com


First Edition March 2005
ISBN 1-933274-05-0

## *Dedication:*

*Call to the Hunt* is dedicated to Sara Kate, who is always ready to watch a monster movie with Daddy.

## *Acknowledgements:*

The author would like to thank the following people:
Kelly Ganson (aka Crow Ravenscar) for being the first to
believe in Shara, Ulrik, their friends and foes
Kelli Dunlap for continued support
Nicole Thomas for giving a lycanthrope a chance
Nathan Barker for second chances
and
Kelley Armstrong for her continued generosity and support

# CALL TO THE HUNT

# CONTENTS

# INTRODUCTION
## Kelley Armstrong

He runs, muzzle sluicing through the cold night air, ears flat against his head, eyes narrowed against the wind. Beneath him, the ground rips past in a brown-gray ribbon. The pound of his paws melds with the thudding of his heart, the sounds indistinguishable. He catches a whiff of rabbit and almost stops, but forces his legs to keep moving. There's something else he's looking for tonight, something better. A moment later, the breeze brings a new smell, something that sets his heart racing double-time, and his paws rushing to match it. He forces himself to slow and sniffs again. Yes, there it is. That musky scent he could never mistake for another. As he changes direction, a sound cuts through the still air and the fur on his back rises. He stops to listen, closes his eyes and drinks it in. Another howl joins the first, then another, and another, a half-dozen voices rising as they sing their irresistible song, their call to the hunt.

That is the call of the werewolf, and humans have responded to it since the dawn of time. Find a culture that has lived in contact with wolves and you almost invariably find tales of the werewolf. Sometimes they are the quiet shapeshifters of shamanistic lore, an expression of our respect for nature, our desire to understand her mysteries and absorb her power. Sometimes they are the stone killers of nightmares, an expression of those parts within ourselves we prefer not to see, to blame on "the monster." Sometimes, as in *Call to the Hunt*, they are both—a blending of the mystery and the power and the violence that is the werewolf.

For the better part of a century, the werewolf has been overshadowed by the suave bloodsuckers of popular fiction. Perhaps we can blame Hollywood. In early motion pictures, it was easy enough to stick a pair of fangs on a man, near impossible to turn one into a wolf. So our collective image of the "man who turns into a wolf" became one of the "man who turns into a hairy man." In that universe, the shapeshifter is often relegated to the role of mindless thug, no match for the allure of the sexy and seductive vampire. While a handful of writers struggled to show the appeal of the werewolf, the average moviegoer could not help but hear "werewolf" and think of brutish killing machines and Lon Chaney in mutton-chops. Hardly the sort of beast they wanted to read about.

As the century drew to a close, special effects finally caught up with the concept of the werewolf and we began to see the true shape of the beast. Now, once again, we have a place for writers like Steven E. Wedel, those who know that this is the true appeal of the werewolf, the dream of the man who becomes the wolf. For a few hours, we can read their stories and lose ourselves in the fantasy. We can smell the night forest, feel the hunger in our bellies, and answer the *Call to the Hunt*.

-- Kelley Armstrong
Author of the *Women of the Otherworld* series

# JOURNEY TO A NEW WORLD

## 1

Gretchen Hundt looked around quickly, saw no one was paying her any attention, and braced herself on the rolling deck of the low-riding ship. With a heave, she sent the contents of her wooden bucket into the sea; the light of a full moon reflected in the swath of human and animal waste, gnawed bones and shredded clothing. The items vanished into the dark waves of the Atlantic Ocean to be hidden forever. Gretchen sighed and dropped the bucket to her side.

"Mrs. Hundt, how are you this evening?"

Gretchen jumped a little, then composed herself and turned to face the man who had silently approached her from behind. "I am fine, thank you, Reverend Meer." She was very conscious of her own heavy German accent, which contrasted with the minister's clipped British speech.

"I have not seen your husband of late. Is he well?"

"He is ill, sir," Gretchen answered. "Nothing serious, but he has been keeping to himself not to upset other passengers. It is his stomach and the waves." She gestured toward her bucket, hoping the minister would assume her husband suffered from seasickness.

"Still, I would think he is not invisible."

"Heavens no, sir. He is not that. I must go. Gar will need his bucket."

"Good day to you, Mrs. Hundt." The minister tipped his tall black hat to her. "My best to your husband."

With a nervous look behind her, Gretchen hurried through a doorway in the ship's forecastle and quickly descended ladders into the darkest part of the ship's hold where barrels and crates were stored. She took a nub of candle from a pocket of her dress, lit it and held it above her head. "Gar? I have come back," she called.

At the edge of the circle of light, the face of a wolf appeared and looked back at her. Even after so many years since he was attacked, seeing her husband as a wolf still sent a tickle of trepidation down Gretchen's back. She shook it off and hurried forward to drop to her knees beside him. She put her arms around his neck and nuzzled him. "Gar, my husband, only two more nights and a day and you will be returned to me. It will be none too soon. Reverend Meer is asking about you."

The wolf whined in response, licking her face.

"Mrs. Hundt, are you down here?" a voice asked from the dark behind them. The wolf slipped silently into the shadows and Gretchen turned, still kneeling, holding her candle high above her. The startled face of a man appeared in the glow. "Upon my soul! Is that a wolf?"

Gar lunged from hiding and fastened his teeth onto the man's throat, bringing him down before he could scream. Gretchen bowed her head and turned her face away, knowing the deed had to be done. No one could know. When the dead man's feet stopped kicking the floor of the main hold, Gretchen looked back. A huge blood stain was spreading beneath the man's body.

"May God grant you peace," Gretchen whispered as the man died in her husband's jaws. "Come Gar, we must hide him. He will provide you with meat until your time is done. That is a relief to me, at least."

Gretchen grabbed the man, a sailor in his early twenties, under one arm. The wolf sank his teeth into the man's other shoulder and together they dragged him behind a stack of crates. In the light of her flickering candle Gretchen studied the pool of blood and the trail leading to the corpse. The ninety-foot ship was just too small. She worried that others would come into the hold filled with supplies the settlers would use to start life in the New World.

"I will come back soon to clean the blood," Gretchen said. Standing over the body, her husband blinked at her. She knew he understood she could not watch him eat the man. "Two dead in as many nights," she said quietly. "People will suspect."

Just before dawn, Gretchen crept back on deck with another bucket filled with bloody water and as many small bones as she dared carry. The watch on deck had changed. Reverend Meer was nowhere to be seen. Gretchen dumped the contents of the bucket over the ship's side, watching as a left hand, chewed from its arm, banged against the wood once before hitting the water. Exhausted, she went back into the hold and found a corner where she could sleep for a few hours.

## 2

Gretchen picked up a chewed, skeletal arm, minus the hand, and placed it in a pile to be bundled and tied with strips of the dead man's clothing. Gar, still suffering the wolf-curse, lay at the edge of the light produced by Gretchen's candle. She gathered the rest of the skeletal remains, leaving the legs that still had bloody meat on them, and tied them tightly together.

The sailor, Benjamin Andrews, had expressed feelings of loneliness and despair to the ship's captain only hours before he found the wolf in the hold. Everyone assumed his despair had gotten the best of him and he'd simply jumped over the side during the night. Gretchen was relieved and kept a prayer of thanks on her lips all during the day. However, belief that a suicide had come the night after a passenger had vanished, presumably from drinking too much rum and tumbling over the side of the ship, had everyone on edge. People were watching one another, wondering who would disappear next.

Gretchen set the bones aside and bent to kiss Gar's snout.

"Tomorrow you will come to me as a man again," she said. "I will be waiting for you on the deck."

She left her husband and climbed the ladder to the deck, the bundle of parts held tightly against her bosom. Early evening stars twinkled overhead and the still-full moon cast much more light than she wished for as she hurried toward the nearest side of the ship. Gretchen lifted the bundle to deliver it to the sea, but the head popped free and bounced away from her across the deck. Still holding the bundle, Gretchen chased the head, but the rocking of the ship rolled it out of her reach. The head bumped into the back of a man's feet.

"What's that?" the man said, turning and looking down.

Gretchen looked up at the man, Jeremiah Smith, and saw his eyes widen at the sight of the head. His gaze traveled from the head to Gretchen's hand stretched toward it, followed her arm to her face, still upturned toward him. His eyes widened further and he looked back to the head, recognition dawning in his features.

"God help us. It's Benjamin Andrews," the man said, taking a step away from the head that had come to rest on the depression where it had once been attached to a neck.

Gretchen lunged for the head, but a strong arm caught her from behind. She was forced down on the deck, the bundle of bones digging into her abdomen. Jeremiah was yelling for Reverend Meers. Soon, a crowd of sailors and settlers had surrounded them. Gretchen tried to hide her face from the confused and horrified stares.

Reverend Meer stepped forward with Abraham Pendle, the ship's captain, and demanded, "What is the meaning of this?"

Jeremiah said, "Reverend, sir, she dropped Benjamin Andrews' head and was chasing it across the deck, sir. Just like a child with a toy. And she has human bones wrapped in the rags beneath her. Upon my word, she does."

Reverend Meer squatted next to the severed head. His face slackened and lost color as he realized how the head was removed. "This man's head has been chewed from the body," he exclaimed. The crowd gasped. "What say you, Mrs. Hundt?"

"I—I have nothing to say, Reverend," Gretchen answered.

"Did you do this?"

Gretchen hung her head without answering.

Reverend Meer asked, "Mrs. Hundt, are you a witch? I accuse you of taking the shape of a werewolf and killing this man. How do you answer that charge?"

"I have nothing to say."

"Ask her where her husband is!"

From where she lay on her back, a man still pressing her flat, Gretchen was just able to see Hannah Hawke standing in the crowd. Like Gretchen, Hannah was going to the New World from Bavaria, with her husband. Their farm had been burned and their home looted in the ongoing religious war. Gretchen and Gar also had lost crops in the long war, but it was Gar's condition that had brought them to the decision to immigrate to the New World. Hannah Hawke was pregnant and kept a hand constantly on the underside of her swollen belly. Her husband, Wilhelm, stood behind her where Hannah demanded answers from Gretchen.

"Did she kill John Mathis, too?" Wilhelm shouted.

The crowd roared and became a manic garden of shaking fists and jeers. They began chanting, "Burn her! Burn her!" Gretchen felt the warm tears sliding down her cheeks. She turned her head away from the mob.

"Hold!" Captain Pendle turned to the crowd, his arms raised to quiet them. "As captain of this ship I tell you there will be no burning. Deal with the witch some other way. I will not have you setting the ship ablaze."

"Saul, you keep her pinned to the deck there," Reverend Meer said to the man on top of Gretchen. "Some of you others, make yourself useful by fetching some rope."

"Please, sir, have mercy," Gretchen begged.

"Save your pleas for the ears of God," the reverend answered. "Lift her up, Saul. Let me see what she holds."

The man holding her tightened his grip around Gretchen's torso, scrabbled to his knees and pulled her up, keeping her feet off the deck. Gretchen clung to the bundle in her arms, but the reverend pulled it from her. She watched him open it and single out a severed arm, bits of meat still clinging to it. His face went pale, then darkened in rage.

"Did you also kill your husband and John Mathis?" he asked through clenched teeth.

"My husband is not dead," Gretchen answered.

"He has been absent for days, Mrs. Hundt. There is nowhere a man can hide on board a ship this small."

"Gar is not dead," Gretchen said again.

"Bind her," Reverend Meer ordered. Men stepped forward and wrapped heavy ropes around Gretchen from shoulders to knees. "For the crimes of witchcraft, werewolfery and murder, we will cast you into the sea, Gretchen Hundt." The reverend looked to the men who had tied her up. "So be it," he said.

"No!" Gretchen screamed as the men picked her up.

"Throw the murderer to the sharks!" Hannah Hawke yelled. "It's better than she deserves." A cheer of agreement went up from the crowd.

"*No!*" Gretchen continued yelling and fighting against her bindings, but it was no use. The heavy rope wrapped around her body pinned her arms to her sides and her lower legs were bound so tightly together she thought the bones might break. As she was lifted over the side of the ship she cursed, "May Gar kill you all!"

The hands released her and she fell into the cold, deep water of the Atlantic.

## 3

Gar awoke in pain. His body was changing shape. After six days as a wolf, he was becoming a man again. He stifled his cries and thought only of holding his wife in human arms. His bones stretched, pulling his skin, softened and reformed, leaving him feeling as if he'd run a hundred miles uphill, but finally he lay still, naked, but a man again, panting in the dark of the hold. After a few moments, he pushed himself to his feet and found the stash of coarse pants, wool shirt and worn leather boots he'd hidden before becoming a wolf. Soft, short wolf hairs floated in the air around him, a byproduct of the change to his human shape.

He climbed the ladders and emerged onto the ship's deck, shielding his eyes from intensely bright sunlight. He was dimly aware of the sound of seagulls coming from somewhere above his head.

"Lord in Heaven!" someone shouted.

Gar squinted at the woman who stared at him in shock, but he couldn't put a name to her terrified face. He wiped a hand across his stubbly face and made for the barrel of fresh water near the mizzenmast. A buzz of conversation followed him. As he lifted his second dipper of water, Gar found himself facing the Puritan minister who'd commissioned the ship for this journey to the New World. He ignored Reverend Meer in his black suit, his battered Bible held at his chest like a shield. He drank his water and hung the dipper on the mast.

"Where have you been, Mr. Hundt?" Meer asked. "We presumed you dead at the hand of your treacherous wife."

"What?" Gar asked. "My wife? Gretchen?"

"She was discovered yesterday trying to dispose of pieces of Benjamin Andrews' body over the side of this ship. We accused her of murdering Mr. Andrews, John Mathis and yourself, as well as the crimes of witchcraft and werewolfery."

"Werewolf?" Gar asked. He could see the minister's knuckles whitening as he gripped his Bible.

"Indeed. The body parts of Mr. Andrews had been gnawed by an animal," Meer said.

"Where is my wife?"

"She was sentenced to death and thrown overboard."

Gar stood still, staring at the minister. He felt his eyes blink a few times, slowly, as he thought about what he'd just heard. "Gretchen is dead? You killed her?"

"She was sentenced to death and thrown overboard," Meer repeated.

"Nooooooooooooooo…" Gar howled. He turned away from the minister and those who had gathered behind him and ran back to the hatch leading below deck. In the darkness of the hold, Gar sobbed, repeating his wife's name over and over. "After so many years of protecting me, the curse placed upon me has killed you, my Gretchen."

He stopped crying. His face became hard. "I'll kill them all."

Gar tore away the clothes he'd just put on and called the wolf to come back to him. He began the change, but stopped at the midway point between wolf and man. This, he knew, was dangerous, as any weapon could kill him while in this in-between stage. And yet, he knew he looked most fearsome at this stage and he was able to maintain the human qualities of walking on two legs while possessing the strength of ten men. He raced for the ladder, where an unlucky sailor had been sent to find him.

Gar tore the sailor from the ladder and snapped off his head in one bite of his massive jaws. As he cast the body aside and returned his attention to the ladder, a voice from high above called out, "Land! Land!" Suddenly confused and unsure how to proceed, Gar slunk back into the shadows of the hold.

Above his head he heard people crowding into the prow of the ship. He let his shape slip back to that of a man. "Land," he whispered. "After so long, Gretchen. Another day and we would have escaped with our secrets."

The anger came back to him, hotter than before, but Gar pushed it away. He would avenge his wife, he vowed, but not yet. Not with land so close at hand.

After a time, he heard more movement on the deck above him. His name was said many times. A shadow filled the opening leading into the hold, then vanished quickly. "Jim's dead," a voice shouted. "His head's done been torn off."

Gar chuckled. He listened to the captain of the ship order men to stand watch over the entrance to the hold, muskets at the ready to shoot anything that tried to come out. Gar lifted his head and howled. Above, women shrieked while men cursed and prayed.

Hours passed. The light streaming into the hold faded, replaced by the soft glow of stars and a waning moon. Gar shifted to his wolf shape and slept fitfully, his canine ears pricked forward, listening for the sound of anyone descending into the ship's hold. He awoke just as early morning sun was returning to the opening. The captain was shouting orders above him. Gar heard the rattle of chains and knew the anchor was being dropped. It was time to make his move.

Still wearing the shape of the wolf, Gar slipped along in the shadows to the ladder. With a rush, he leapt from the hold to the deck, landing on one of the men left to guard the opening. The man's musket fired as he toppled to the deck. A woman gasped and fell as the stray musket ball buried itself in her chest. Gar tore the guard's throat away, his face splashed with flying blood. He turned and jumped on the other guard who had been distracted by the activity of dropping anchor and was struggling to ready his musket as he watched his friend die. Gar brought the man down and killed him quickly.

"I knew they were devils!" a woman screamed. Gar looked up to see Hannah Hawke pointing at him from the quarterdeck. The captain and the minister flanked her, their faces slack with fear. Gar considered rushing them and bringing them down, tasting their flesh and swallowing their blood. He heard more shouts behind him and turned to see dozens of settlers and sailors watching him.

Behind them, a forested shore filled the horizon. Gar froze, transfixed by this first view of the New World, the place where he and Gretchen were to flee from their old life, living in the virgin forest where he could become a wolf without fearing his neighbors. He looked back to Hannah Hawke; she and her husband came from a village not far from the farm Gar had shared with Gretchen. He bared his teeth at her, then jumped over the side of the ship and swam for the shore.

"Shoot him!" the captain and minister shouted in unison. The pop of a few muskets filled the air and Gar heard a pair of lead balls splash into the water around him. He ignored them, knowing the lead couldn't seriously hurt him, and swam the short distance to the beach.

Once on land, he turned for a last look at the ship, then ran into the woods, not stopping until the smell of the sea was gone from his nostrils. Finally, he fell to the leaf-carpeted earth and changed his shape again. With his human form came more tears for his lost wife. He pushed himself to a sitting position and rested his back against the thick trunk of a tree.

"I am alone in a strange land reports say are filled with savages," he said aloud, thinking maybe somehow, somewhere, Gretchen would still hear him.

As a man alone in an unfamiliar setting, he knew he would be weak and virtually helpless. The wolf, though… the wolf would feel right at home. With a sigh, Gar called the wolf back to him and allowed himself to change shape again. He stood on four legs and sniffed the air; the smell of game was varied and thick. The wolf grinned and padded away.

# 4

Gar crouched low to the ground and peered warily from the shady darkness of a fragrant green shrub on the edge of a clearing in the woods. The clearing was occupied by a village of native people. For several days he had watched them work and play. He knew they'd seen him; after a few days, he'd deliberately shown himself to them in wolf form. Instead of trying to drive him away or running in fear, the small knot of dark-skinned people had pointed and spoke to one another in low, reverent tones. After a few moments had passed, Gar turned and went deeper into the woods. But, he always found himself coming back to the edge of this village to watch the New World natives go about their daily activities.

The men wore breeches of animal skin and strings of beads covered their chests. The women wore dresses made of animal skin, each with a blanket draped from her left shoulder to her right hip. Young children ran naked. The houses were made of mud with flat roofs, low doorways covered with weighted animal hides and no windows. Smoke often curled from a hole in the center of the roofs.

As Gar watched now, many men sat together stringing bows and tying stone heads to arrows. Women tended to meat cooking over a large open fire made near the center of the village. Gar was hungry.

As the sun sank in the west, the natives assembled in a circle around the large fire. Several men sat in the shadows beyond the light of the flame and began beating a drum. An Indian dressed in a wolf skin entered the circle between the drummers and the fire and began to dance, making arm gestures toward the sky, the ground and the surrounding forest. Three more Indians joined the first, one of them naked, his hands bound behind his back and his ankles tied; the other two carried him as he struggled. The tied Indian was dropped on the ground before the dancing Indian dressed as a wolf. The men watching raised their weapons and whooped.

The dancer struck a menacing pose over the bound man, then lifted his head and howled, his arms uplifted. Then he resumed dancing around the fire, seeming to ignore the captive.

Gar thought about the earlier activity of preparing weapons. He wondered if the village was preparing for war. He suspected that the bound man must be a captured enemy. And, judging by the way the Indians had looked at him and the dancing of the man in the wolf skin, he guessed they saw the wolf as a god or a demon. Either way, the wolf was a special animal to them.

Deciding to act rather than attempt to analyze the situation further, Gar stood and left his hiding place, walking slowly as he advanced on the group. A surprised call went up as the first villagers saw him. Indians backed away from him as he approached, their faces filled with awe. The drums stopped. The village became silent. Gar approached the dancer and stopped before him.

Gar hesitated only a moment, wondering if he was about to die. He looked into the dark eyes of the native, saw only wonder, and made his decision. He changed his shape to the half-man and paused again so they would all see it and comprehend the transformation, then he finished it, becoming a naked white man among the Indians. As a body, they scrambled away from him, their heads lowered in reverence. The dancer fell to his knees, putting his head in the dirt at Gar's feet.

Gar looked around him. The men who had been gathered around the fire all stood back at a distance, their heads lowered. Behind them were the women, also with bowed heads, many holding their children. The children gaped at him, their dark eyes seeming even darker in the flickering firelight.

"I will be your god," Gar shouted, knowing they would not understand him, but feeling compelled to make some bold statement.

He changed shape again and approached the bound man. He saw heads lifting; all eyes were fixed on him. The bound man stared at him in terror and tried to roll away but he was caught between the wolf and the fire. He screamed. Gar locked his teeth into the man's throat.

All around him, the Indians sent up a cheer and waved their weapons. Gar lifted his head and howled. The men of the village rushed forward and hacked at the bound man with stone axes and knives, pulling off parts of the body and eating the raw flesh.

Gar sensed the men being filled with bloodlust as they gorged themselves on the raw human meat. They shouted at one another, pounded their chests and brandished spears. Their faces and chests became smeared crimson with blood as they ate. At a call from the man wearing the wolf skin, the men let out a whoop and ran into the forest.

Gar ran after them. They ran for a long time, until another village came into sight. Gar could not tell that the people living in this village were so much different than those he traveled with, but his group fell on them as if they were a coven of vermin that had to be cleansed from the earth.

Men emerged from the doorways of the flat-roofed houses, let out yells and grabbed weapons to rush out and meet the battle. Women and children screamed. Arrows and spears flew in every direction, many finding homes in the bodies of the invaders and the invaded. Gar ran among the men living in the invaded village, slashing with his fangs, killing some and sending many more fleeing in terror.

Then, as suddenly as it had begun, the fight was over. The Indians he came with turned and raced away. Gar ran with them rather than behind them now, back through the dark forest to their own homes.

14

Back in the first village, the tall Indian who wore the wolf skin left the group of men and approached Gar. All around them, the other warriors watched eagerly, their eyes glinting in the fire the women kept burning. Several of the men who left the village did not return, Gar noted. The wolf-clad Indian spoke in his native language, motioning to one of the houses. Gar swiftly changed to his human shape and answered the Indian.

"I do not know what you are saying," Gar said. "But if you are offering me shelter, I accept it. If you are luring me into a trap, I will kill you."

The Indian led Gar to the door of the house, then stepped away, motioning for Gar to go inside. Gar entered and found a small fire burning in the middle of the floor, the smoke rising and exiting through a hole in the roof. Piles of furry skins were laid out in a bed. A table held a rough cup and a serving of steaming meat. Gar turned toward his host, but the Indian had backed away, letting the hide door fall over the opening to the house. Gar sat and began to eat.

# 5

Two months later, Gar, dressed in breeches made of deerskin, sat cross-legged on the ground before a fire near the center of the village. Behind him, two warriors stood at attention, their arms crossed over their chests. A woman poured liquid from a large pitcher into a cup at Gar's side.

Since his first night among the villagers, who called themselves the Chawana, Gar had learned some of their language, had helped them in three more skirmishes, feasted with them, danced with them and let them worship him as man and wolf.

But he longed for the face of another white soul. He ached for his Gretchen, refusing offers to take various Chawana women into his hut. He wanted the company of someone who knew he was no god, only a man cursed to become a wolf for six days each month.

He drank from the cup at his side, then stood and addressed his guards. "I will come back. Do not follow me," he said. As the Indians looked from him to one another in confusion, Gar hurried into the forest. He traveled for several days toward the rising sun, staying in his human form despite it being slower than traveling as a wolf. Finally, he emerged from the forest to face the shore and the rolling ocean. He followed the coast north to the place where he'd swum ashore from the ship that had carried him to the New World.

The ship was gone, but Gar easily found where the passengers had disembarked and trekked northeast from the shore. He soon came to a large clearing, made larger by the harvesting of the trees that had stood around its edges. A cluster of cabins stood in the clearing, with a lane running down the center of them. To the north of the settlement, Puritan men were cutting down more trees to use for construction and firewood and to clear land for crops. To the south, women and children tended a newly plowed garden.

Gar crept into the village, looking into the window of the first cabin he came to. It was furnished with a small table, two chairs and a bed in one corner. Cooking utensils hung near the hearth. Hannah Hawke, no longer pregnant, was putting an iron pot over a fire in the hearth. Gar moved away from the window, slipping around to the front of the cabin. He stopped dead in his tracks with one foot raised to step onto the low porch.

A cradle squatted beside the open door of the cabin. He could see a baby wrapped in blankets sleeping soundly within the cradle. Gar stared for a long time, many thoughts flitting through his mind. The child was beautiful, with full, healthy cheeks and a crown of dark hair. A tiny fist had slipped from the blankets to rest near the baby's face. Gretchen had delivered three children in her life, Gar thought. Two were born dead and the third died in his father's arms two days after she was born.

He remembered learning Gretchen had been accused of his crimes. She'd been thrown overboard, to drown, to have her dead flesh eaten by the fish because of him.

Hannah Hawke had accused him even as he fled the ship, Gar recalled, seeing the woman's face, twisted in hate and fear, one arm outstretched to point accusingly at him while the other hand rested on her swollen belly, holding the unborn child he now saw before him.

The sound of several men speaking reminded Gar where he was. He took a last look at the sleeping child, then edged back around the house and hurried to the shadows of the woods. He stayed there, pacing among the trees, fighting with his thoughts of hatred, of envy, of revenge.

When night fell, he decided he would act. Lights burned within the log homes of the settlers. Gar removed his clothes and silently made his way back to the home of Wilhelm and Hannah Hawke. He stepped onto the porch made of new lumber and paused a moment at the closed wooden door. Inside, he could hear Hannah singing softly to the baby. He sniffled and determined that Wilhelm also was inside the cabin. Gar closed his eyes and remembered Hannah pointing at him, accusing him as she must have done in helping to condemn his Gretchen to death.

He called the wolf, freezing the transformation at the mid-point. With a roar, he crashed through the door of the cabin. Wilhelm jumped from a chair at the table. Gar swung a thick, hairy arm at the man's head and felt the skull cave in while the neck snapped. Wilhelm fell to the floor, dead before his bleeding face hit the freshly planed lumber. Hannah was screaming, standing beside the cradle, bent over, unsure how to protect her infant. Gar advanced on her slowly, baring his teeth so he would appear as menacing as he possibly could.

He watched Hannah's eyes flit from him to the crushed doorway to her crying baby. She made a dash for the open door, leaving the child in his cradle. Gar snatched her as she tried to dart around him. He lifted her off her feet and brought her face close to his. He let the wolf slip away just enough to allow speech.

"You know who I am?" he asked. She nodded, too scared to remember to scream. Gar let the wolf come back. He clamped his teeth in Hannah's left shoulder until he felt the bones crack. He tore away a mouthful of meat and bone, swallowed it, and tore away the woman's throat. He feasted until he felt her go limp and die in his grasp, then he dropped her to the floor and turned his attention to the crying baby.

He changed shape, becoming fully human again before he stepped beside the cradle; a shower of gray and white wolf hair fell from his body to the floor of the cabin. Outside, he could hear people calling to one another, asking where the screaming had come from. Gar glanced quickly at the open doorway, then carefully lifted the baby from the cradle. He turned and ran for the woods.

In the cover of the trees, Gar held the infant close to his naked chest until the baby quieted.

"Hush now," Gar said. "I will be your father now. I will raise you as my own and give you the gift I have. You will have two names. The Chawana will call you Magwa, skin-changer. I will call you Ulrik, which means wolf ruler. You will do great things in your life."

# OF WITCHES AND WEREWOLVES

Frances Cavendish stood back, at the edge of the crowd, his head bowed, studying his dusty shoes. Occasionally somebody jostled him, moving by to get a closer look. Voices swirled in the air like autumn leaves, dead and somber, memories of summer past and promises of a winter to come. Frances looked up, a tall man, he was able to see over the bonnets and hats of the throng between him and the gallows. The victims were in place, the ropes around their necks.

"What is this?"

Startled by the voice, Frances turned to see who had spoken. A tall young man with a full beard, shoulder-length black hair and thick eyebrows had come to stand beside him. The man was dressed in buckskin. "Josef," Frances said in greeting. "Another hanging. Witches."

"Witches?" Josef Ulrik turned his eyes from Frances to the gallows and back. "Those women?"

"They have been accused, tried and convicted."

"You said 'another hanging.' There have been others?"

"This is the third in four months," Frances answered. "The women you see yonder, Goody Cotton and her daughter Chloe, will be the eighth and ninth people hanged for witchcraft since…"

"Since what?"

"I dare not say."

"Your manner says you have doubts about their guilt."

Frances pulled his eyes from the women weeping on the wooden platform and back to his companion. "See how the accused are not taunted? Nothing is being thrown at them as they stand ready to die for the crimes they are accused of? The voices of those gathered to witness the executions are hushed, somber. Well they should be. Who knows which of us might stand before the town with a rope about our necks tomorrow?"

"You must tell me more of this," Josef said.

Frances nodded, wishing he had the skills to live as Josef did, away from the village—some even said he lived among the Indians—trapping and hunting for the things he needed, coming into the village only to trade furs. "Yes," he said. "I would gladly tell you. Will you join me for dinner tonight? My daughter makes the best cherry pie in the New World."

"I will be there," Josef said, his eyes still on the gallows.

"I daresay Emily will take extra care with her baking knowing that you will be joining us," Frances said, glancing behind him to the doorway of the shop where Emily had retreated earlier, unwilling to witness the death of her friend Chloe.

The executioner, Matthew Poe, was positioning the doomed women at the edge of the platform, ready to push them over.

"I cannot watch this," Frances said. He turned his back to the scene. Beside him, Josef continued to watch. The voices of the crowd were stilled. Only the weeping of the condemned, and the pleas of their husband and father, could be heard. Frances closed his eyes, unable to bear the desperate sound of Nathaniel Cotton's entreaties for mercy. A choked yell came from the gallows, followed by another. Nathaniel screamed. And then another voice, shrill and angry, filled the air.

"See the witches die!" Winona Buckley screamed. Frances opened his eyes and turned to see the slight, grimy figure of the woman at the front of the crowd. She waved her arms and paced between the spectators and the gallows where the bodies still twitched as they dangled in their nooses, wisps of graying hair flying around the blue bonnet she wore on her head. "Were they godly women, the Lord would not allow them to die. You know this. May all the witches of Haven take notice of the justice of the Lord!"

She continued to rave, but Frances could stand no more. "Come to my home at dusk. I can bear no more of this," he said to his friend, then hurried into the shop where his daughter's tear-stained face was watching from a window. Frances led Emily through the shop and out the back door and quickly to the small house they shared.

As the sun faded from the sky, a knock came at the door of the Cavendish house. Frances glanced at his daughter and saw her smile for the first time in many days as she looked toward the door. She quickly ran her hands over her apron, smoothing wrinkles that were not there, and raised a hand to make sure no hair had come loose from its bindings. Her blue eyes danced with more light than what was provided by the fire in the hearth and the two lanterns.

"Father, our guest has arrived," she said.

"So he has," Frances agreed, rising from his chair. He wasn't sure he approved of his daughter's affection for the mysterious woodsman, but if it took her mind from the tragedy of the day, he would endure it in silence. He opened the door and shook hands with Josef as he entered. "You remember my daughter, Emily," Frances said, gesturing toward the girl, who gave her best curtsy.

"One does not forget such a face," Josef said, bowing in return. Emily giggled and turned away quickly.

"Come, Josef, sit here at the table while Emily finishes preparing dinner."

"Your house smells as if the king's own chefs were at work at the stove," Ulrik said. From her place at the hearth, Emily giggled again.

The two men sat at the table. Emily put mugs of cider before them, not meeting the eyes of the guest. Frances and Josef drank.

"What I saw today made me very angry," Josef said as he put down his mug. "Those women were not witches. And the man, the husband and father…" Josef shook his shaggy head. "He had to be restrained by several men while that woman, the thin hag, raved about witches in this village. Who is she?"

"Winona Buckley," Frances answered. "She brought the accusations. She brought all the accusations against those who have died on the gallows these past months. Life in Haven has been very tense since she arrived from Salem. She says her husband was murdered by witches and she came here because she could not bear to remain in Salem. Soon, however, she said Haven was no more free of witchcraft than Salem. John Franklin's milk cow died. Winona said witches killed it. She said young Ruth Willow was the witch.

"Ruth was the first to stand on the gallows. Her friends and neighbors hurled insults, vegetables and stones at her before she was pushed off and… and died."

"And the others?" Josef asked.

"At first, Winona blamed those she accused for various things we could see, like the death of a cow. Then she said the spirits of living women were attacking her in her home as she tried to sleep. Those women were hanged."

"Did they confess?"

"Two of them did, as they stood upon the gallows," Frances said. "They were desperate, begging for their lives. During the trial, Winona claimed the women were sending their spirits to attack her right there in the courtroom. She thrashed about and fell on the floor as if she were under attack. It was convincing."

"But you think it was a show?"

"I do!" Emily said as she put plates of food before the men. "I think she wants to see all the women in town who are prettier than her put to death so that she may have her pick of the men."

"Hush, child. Hush," Frances said. "Do not speak so."

"You do not deny your daughter's claim," Josef said.

Frances looked at his guest for a long moment. "No, I do not. Will you lead the blessing of the food, Josef."

"It is your house, Frances. I wish that you would say the blessing."

Frances bowed his head and quickly thanked God for the food they were about to eat. He and Josef both filled their mouths. Josef motioned toward Emily and asked Frances, "Please, allow your daughter to join us. There is no need for her to wait for the men to finish before she eats."

"If you wish it," Frances agreed. Blushing, Emily came to the table and hesitantly began eating with the men.

"What of the women who died today?" Josef asked. "What were their crimes."

Frances paused and glanced at Emily. He was about to answer, but his daughter boldly spoke first.

"Winona Buckley said they were werewolves."

Josef lowered his fork and knife, looked from Emily to Frances. Frances nodded. Josef suddenly threw back his head and roared with laughter. After a moment, he regained his composure, but his eyes danced with mirth. "I am very sorry," he said, directing the apology mostly at Emily, who appeared about to weep. "Truly I am," Josef said, his tone now more sincere. "It is just such an absurd claim. Who would believe that those women who were hanged today were werewolves? Did somebody see them change their shapes?"

"Only Winona," Frances answered. "She said she saw them take on the form of wolves when she went to the creek to wash her clothes. She said that before the women changed shape she heard them discussing how they would meet the devil in the woods and…" Frances glanced at his daughter and saw that her eyes were moist. "And copulate with him."

"It isn't true," Emily said sharply.

"Of course it is not," Josef said. "Those women were no more werewolves than you or your father."

They ate in silence for a moment. "This woman, Winona Buckley, where does she live?" Josef asked.

"Off the main road leading out of town to the east," Frances asked. "There is a small cabin with a windmill. The windmill is in ill repair and unused, but Winona lives in the cabin. Why do you ask?"

"Only curious," Josef answered. He ate the last bite of roasted pork and looked at Emily. "Now, my lady, I have heard legends concerning your cherry pie and I would know if they are true."

After the meal, the men retired to the porch and smoked pipes. The crescent moon was high in the night sky when Josef rose to take his leave. "It was good of you to come," Frances said. "I hope you will come again. I know Emily would enjoy it."

"But you do not think I am the right man for her, do you Frances?"

Frances sighed and looked away, across the street to the field of corn he would have to tend tomorrow. "We know so little of you, Josef. You seem like a good man, but I do not even know where you make your home. I could not approve of you calling on my daughter without knowing more about you."

"Soon, I think, you will know a great deal about me," Josef said. "And then I think you will not wish to see me again. Good evening, Frances. Please bid your lovely daughter farewell for me."

Without waiting for a response, Josef rose and walked briskly away down the road, heading east. Frances finished his pipe, wondering at the strange good-bye, then went inside. Emily was visibly sad to learn their guest had left without speaking directly to her again, but smiled that he had left a message with her father. Within an hour, both Frances and his daughter were snugly in their beds and sleeping.

They were awakened by the sound of howling.

Frances sat up in bed and found Emily in his bedroom doorway. "What is it, Father?" she asked, her voice trembling.

"Wolves," Frances answered, throwing aside the blankets and getting out of bed. His dressing gown flapped around his shins as he hurried from the room. "They sound close. Like they're right in town."

He stopped in the main room of the house and listened closer to the wild sound filling the night. Frances looked at his daughter, who stood near the table, her hands clenched under her chin. "It is only one," Frances said. "One wolf. It is moving through town from the east, coming this way."

"Will you load the musket?"

"Yes. Yes." Frances went back to his bedroom and took his musket from the pegs above the doorway. He hadn't used the long rifle in months, having no need to hunt. It had a thin film of dust covering it. He pulled off his nightcap and began wiping away the dust with the cap as he returned to the main room. Emily held his powder horn and bag of lead balls extended toward him. The howling was closer.

"Hurry Father."

"There likely is no reason to fear," Frances said, taking the powder and shot. "He is moving steadily, not stopping to do mischief. Probably he will pass right by and return to the forest."

Frances began the process of readying the gun for firing. As he pushed the rod down the barrel to pack his shot, he stopped. The wolf was in the street before his house. The howling stopped. Frances looked toward the front window. The window was covered by lace curtains made by his wife Martha only months before she died trying to bring a second child into the home. Frances looked to Emily and saw that her eyes, too, were fixed on the window.

They both jumped when the snuffling sound came from the other side of the glass. Frances wished he had closed the shutters, but they were open. Nothing stood between them and the wolf but the thin panes of glass.

"Father—"

Emily was cut off by another howl, so loud it shook the glass in the window and filled the house with a sound like rushing, mournful wind. Frances pulled the rod from his rifle and lifted the gun to his shoulder. He had to concentrate to keep the tip of the barrel steady. "Emily, go beside the window and tear down the curtains. Do it sudden. I will shoot the beast through the glass, but I must see the devil to hit it."

Moving slowly, Emily went to stand between the window and the front door. She reached out with a small pale hand, gripped the lace as the snuffling sound resumed, and jerked hard, screaming and turning away as she did.

Frances forgot to fire the musket. He raised his face from the sights, his eyes wide, his mouth working. "Dear God in Heaven," he said.

On the other side of the window was a huge black wolf, standing on its hind legs, its black nose pressed to the glass, its eyes boring into Frances and an expression like a grin spreading its lips. But on its head was the distinctive blue bonnet of Winona Buckley. The wolf raised its head and howled again, then dropped to all fours and jumped off the porch. It returned to the street and raced back down the road, heading east.

"What was it, Father? Why didn't you shoot?"

"I... it..." Frances pulled his eyes from the window and looked at his daughter. "It was no ordinary wolf. It wore a bonnet. It wore Winona Buckley's bonnet."

"Winona Buckley?" Emily raised her hands to cover her mouth.

"I must get dressed," Frances said. "I will dress and close the shutters. The men will be gathering. I must go."

By the time Frances reached the center of town, Winona Buckley had been caught and brought to the church in iron chains. Her trial was to be held immediately and all who had seen the wolf were summoned to testify. Frances entered the church and took his place in a pew. Despite it being three in the morning, the sanctuary was nearly full of men, women and children in various states of dress, but all wide awake and frightened. Winona Buckley sat in a chair behind a table at the front of the sanctuary. At the pulpit, Reverend Howard Matheson sat with the other church elders. Howard rapped on the surface of his table and called for order.

"Winona Buckley," the reverend called. "You are accused of witchcraft and werewolfery. How do you plead."

"I was attacked," the small woman screamed. "He came to me in my house and—"

"How do you plead?" Howard roared over her.

"I am not guilty, Reverend," she replied. Three rows back, Frances heard the fear in her voice.

A dozen men came forward and told how they'd seen the wolf in town after being awakened by its howling, how they'd looked out their windows and seen the beast wearing Winona's bonnet and how when the wolf ran back through town, going east, they had followed at a safe distance.

"We found a slaughtered calf laying on the ground outside her front door," Phillip Stevenson said. "It's throat had been torn open by a wolf. We burst through her door and found Winona Buckley cowering in a corner. She was naked and the room was full of these hairs." He raised his fist and opened it, letting a cascade of fine, short wolf hairs drift toward the floor. "Like she had just turned back to her human form. We made her get dressed and we brought her here."

In his turn, Frances rose and told his tale of being awakened by the wolf and how he had seen the animal looking back at him through the window of his home. When the accusations were finished, the minister turned back to Winona and asked, "How do you answer these charges?"

"He came to me, like a devil," she said. "He walked like a man but looked like a wolf. Naked, he was, and covered in the black hair. He pulled me from my bed, tore away my clothes and tied me up. He left me on the floor, put on my bonnet and then, I swear it, he dropped to his hands and became a big wolf. God save me, but he did. Then he ran out the front door. He returned just before these men and untied me, then ran back out."

The minister studied the woman for a long moment. "Many people have been put to death in Haven since your arrival, Winona Buckley," he said. "You accused them of witchcraft, but now I think that you blinded this court and lay your own crimes on those this court sent to death. It is not a Christian attitude, and yet I take great pride in knowing that with this sentence of death I give some measure of vengeance to those who have already died in your stead."

"No!" she shrieked. Winona Buckley continued screaming until she was taken from the building and confined in the store-house that had served as a prison to those she had accused.

Howard looked over the assembled witnesses and wiped his brow. "May God forgive us for what we have done in the past and bless what we are about to do. The guilty will be hanged until dead at noon this day. Go to your homes and get what sleep you can before returning to witness God's justice on this evil creature."

Frances left the church and hurried home. The sky was turning pink on the eastern horizon. Dawn was approaching, and with it would be the start of the day's chores. There would be no time for sleep. He knocked on his door and waited for Emily to call out to ask who was there, then she let him in.

They sat at the table and ate a breakfast of bread and salt pork as Frances told about the trial of Winona Buckley. "I am sorry I did not send word back to tell you what was happening," he said.

"That's all right, Father," Emily said. "Josef Ulrik told me the trial was being held immediately."

"Josef? He was here?"

"Yes. He left this for you." Winona went to the hearth and returned with a small bundle of rabbit pelts bound with string.

"What is the meaning of this?" Frances asked, studying the rolled bundle. "Why did you open the door to him, or to anyone other than me?"

"He is a friend of yours," Emily said. "I thought we could trust him."

"Did he say anything? Why didn't he come to the trial? Why was he in town? Did he see the wolf?"

"I do not know," Emily said, but her face suddenly burned scarlet.

"He said something that causes you to blush," Frances said.

"It was quite strange," Emily admitted. "He brought the furs and asked me to give them to you. He said you would find them most interesting. Then he, well, if you must know, he kissed my hand and said the most peculiar thing. He said that if I ever wanted to leave the path and dance with him in the forest that he would be there, waiting for me."

"That is intolerable," Frances said. "I will not have him talking to my daughter that way. What did you say to him?"

"I told him such talk was not proper. I said only devils and Indians dance in the forest," Emily said. "He laughed like he did at supper yesterday. He laughed and said I would not see him in Haven again, then he kissed my hand and left."

"Intolerable," Frances said again. "And to think I gave the man the benefit of the doubt when so many others accuse him of being as wild as the cannibal Indians he is known to consort with."

Frances took up his knife and cut the string holding the furs. The pelts fell away and both he and his daughter gasped in shock at what was revealed in the heart of the bundle. With a trembling hand, Frances lifted Winona Buckley's blue bonnet from the pile of furs. Thin black wolf hairs fell away from the bonnet, drifting lazily to the table.

"Father, what does it mean?" Emily asked. "What does it mean?"

# THE FEAST OF SARATOGA

*"We hear this huge sound, like the howling of dogs. At first we think it's a trick of the enemy, so we send out a detachment to reconnoit.*
*"They come back and report to us—it's wolves. One sets up a cry when it finds a corpse, then the others join it in that hideous sound as they rip it apart.*
*"The howling gets louder and louder."*
— From the diary of Sgt. Rodger Lamb, HMRA Oct. 1777

The distant sound of popping muskets filled the evening, but Colonel Josef Ulrik didn't trouble himself with them; they were too far away for him to care. Occasionally there was the roar of cannon, but that, too, was a sound from a distant battle. Ulrik remained crouched behind a massive elm tree and watched a line of red-coated British troops moving along the road toward Saratoga in the New York colony. The soldiers marched stiffly, confidently, but some of them showed fear in their eyes. Some even looked toward the dark forests on either side of the road, as if thinking about what was lurking in the shadows. The colonel grinned.

The last British soldier passed. Ulrik waited until the man was ready to turn a corner before motioning at the Indian hiding behind the next tree. The dark-skinned warrior nodded, then lifted his head and gave a short, harsh call, like a turkey, and the forest shadows came to life with red men who went slinking beside the road, keeping the end of the British column in view.

Near nightfall, the British troops claimed lodging at a farmhouse. Ulrik watched from the forest as the leader of the troops, a lieutenant, sent the farm wife scurrying to supply the necessities for his camp of about fifty men. The lieutenant remained in the house while his men pitched tents around the barn. The moon rose above the trees. British guards moved away from the body of the encampment to act as sentries.

Around him, Ulrik felt his Indian troops fanning out to keep the sentries in sight. He sat motionless, watching the log cabin and the barn behind it. Occasionally he saw dark shapes moving behind the yellow squares of lighted windows. The smell of cooking meat rose with the smoke from the chimney. Sometimes he heard men laughing. He waited.

General Horatio Gates had sent Ulrik and the Indian detachment to patrol this road and delay any British troops using it. These redcoats, Ulrik knew, were on their way to join the forces of General John Burgoyne. Ulrik had received word that morning that Gates was entrenched on Bemis Heights, a narrow place between the hills and Hudson River on the road to Albany. Burgoyne had been stopped about a mile north, on the Freeman farm, by Colonel Daniel Morgan. Ulrik's duty was to make sure the redcoats he was watching never joined Burgoyne.

After four hours, the British sentries were replaced. Three more hours later, Ulrik heard the low chitter of a raccoon to his right. The call was followed by a sound like an axe striking wood. To his left he heard a grunt that ended in a gurgle. The sentries closest to him were dead; he could smell their blood. A few moments later and he heard several more mimicked animal sounds, indicating that all the sentries had been successfully killed.

Ulrik smiled and nodded. He lifted his head and sounded a perfect imitation of the wolf's mournful howl. The call was answered from all sides.

Like ghosts, the Indians moved away from the farm, slipping silently past Ulrik. He could smell their fear and hear the nervousness in their quick footfalls. Soon, he was alone, but only for a moment.

New shapes approached the farmhouse—low, fast forms that did not have fear in their steps. The wolves came silently, sliding around the trees like spirits of the damned. One, a large gray wolf with a gleaming crescent scar on his muzzle, paused and stared at Ulrik. The animal's tail was up. He lowered it as he faced the man.

"Go on, my friend," Ulrik urged. "Go to your feast. I promise you there will be more to come."

The animal flicked its tongue out, sliding it along his jaw, then turned and vanished. Already, Ulrik could hear the sounds of wolves feeding on the warm bodies of the sentries. He got to his feet and slipped away to rejoin the Indians.

Ulrik slept for three hours. When he awoke, the British troops already had left the little farm in the woods. Ulrik sent the Indians on to follow the soldiers and started toward the house.

A woman pulled aside the curtain covering a window next to the door when he knocked. She held a long knife in the hand she used to move the curtain. She looked at Ulrik, then at the land around her home. The curtain fell back and a moment later the door opened a crack.

"What do you want?" she asked.

"I am Colonel Josef Ulrik. I serve under General Horatio Gates. I would talk to you about the British soldiers who camped here last night."

The woman eyed him suspiciously for a long moment, then opened the door and moved aside. Ulrik stepped into the cabin. The woman leaned out the doorway and looked around again, then slammed the door closed.

"You knew they were here?" she asked.

"Yes."

"And you didn't do anything? Why didn't you attack them and drive them off?"

Ulrik glanced around the house. A boy of about eleven lay on a bed in one corner of the cabin. His left eye was bruised and there was a deep oozing scratch on his right cheek. The boy was asleep. Beside his bed stood a small girl Ulrik guessed to be six years old.

"They would have killed you all had we attacked," Ulrik answered. "Also, I have only a dozen Delaware Indians with me. Would you rather host the Indians?"

"No." She tried to meet his gaze and couldn't.

"Did they hurt you?"

"Not me. They hurt my son. An officer hit him when Daniel said… when he said his father would kill them all for breaking into our house."

"Your husband is in the militia?"

31

The woman glanced sidelong at the children. The girl was facing them, one fist over her mouth, her eyes like large blue moons. "He was," the woman said as she looked back to Ulrik. "A letter came two weeks ago saying he was k-k-k—"

"I understand," Ulrik said. "I am very sorry. You have a brave son. Take comfort in that, and that these redcoats did no more harm than they did.

"What can you tell me of their supplies?" he asked. "Did they speak of it? Did they take food or ammunition from you? Did you hear them speak of their orders or destination?"

"We had a powder horn and a musket. An old one. They took both," she said. "They had me baking all night and took all the bread I made, and all the meat in the smokehouse. They didn't say anything about where they were going. Not that I heard."

"I see."

"They were going to take all our chickens, but they left in a hurry," the woman said. "The wolves came in the night and killed their sentries. The wolves... ate the men. That seemed to spook the soldiers. I got the impression the wolves have been following them for a long time. Perhaps you and your Indian friends should learn to kill like the wolves."

"Perhaps." Ulrik smiled. "Perhaps we will learn that lesson." He glanced again at the children, then back to the woman, and nodded. "Since you have your chickens still, I trust you will have enough meat and eggs for the time being. I will leave you now."

He left the cabin and started down the porch steps.

"Wait!" The woman ran out of the cabin and clutched at his arm. Ulrik stopped and faced her. Her lips were pursed, her brow furrowed as she looked for the words she wanted. "They killed my husband. He was at Ticonderoga. I want you to... will you..." Her eyes watered. She turned her face away.

Ulrik knew the little girl was standing in the doorway, watching them. He took the woman's chin in his large hand and turned her tear-streaked face up to his. "I assure you, I will make these soldiers suffer for what their countrymen have done to your husband," he promised. He released her and walked quickly away from the farm.

He caught up with the Indians at about noon. Thirty minutes later he was slipping along with them, watching the British troops. The soldiers were scared. Ulrik could almost taste their fear. They cast many furtive glances to the right and left of the road, as if expecting the wolves to come charging at them in broad daylight.

Fools, Ulrik thought. I would be scared too, if I was foolish enough to march arrogantly along the roadway through hostile territory.

Makua, one of the Indians, came up beside Ulrik and whispered to him that there was an area about two miles ahead where the white man's road passed the bottom of a wooded hill.

"We could kill many soldiers from the trees above and be gone before they find us," Makua said.

Ulrik nodded and gave the word for the Indians to proceed ahead of the soldiers. He remained behind to be sure the British troops did not deviate from their course. The soldiers soon approached the hill. Ulrik saw that Makua had been right—the road passed round the base of the hill, with a sheer rock cliff rising about seventy-five feet above the west side of the road. Dense woods stood all along the top of the cliff.

The soldiers sensed that it would be a good place for an ambush. They stopped. Ulrik watched the lieutenant confer with two other men. A third man was called forward, then dispatched ahead.

Ulrik slipped further into the cover of trees. He raised his head and gave the wolf call again. He was answered from all around. As the animal sounds faded, Ulrik could hear the excited talk of the soldiers back on the road. They were truly afraid now.

Ulrik crept back to the road and moved even with the head of the waiting column. He knelt beside an oak tree that shone brilliantly in its fall foliage. Acorns dug into his knee and a few fat, crisp leaves floated past his face. He leveled his long musket, aiming for the lieutenant, a tall man with blond hair and crooked teeth. Ulrik pulled the musket's hammer back and squeezed the trigger.

He vanished into the woods before the lieutenant's body hit the ground. Only a small cloud of musket smoke gave away where he had been. As he moved away, he called to the wolves again and they answered. Ulrik stopped and listened. He could hear the soldiers moving, but they weren't coming after him. They were moving south again, toward the hill and the waiting Indians. Ulrik started after them.

Makua ordered the Indians to fire sooner than they should have. Ulrik wished they had waited until the center of the line was under the cliff. As it was, they fired when the first redcoats were below them. Ulrik counted six British soldiers slumping to the ground as the echo of the volley bounced through the woods.

The remaining soldiers fired back, aiming at the woods above them, unable to see the Indians. Then they broke and ran in a most unorderly fashion. Ulrik grinned. Such a charge was not practiced in British training drills. The redcoats ran past the cliff and around the bend in the road. Ulrik followed.

Twice more during that day, Ulrik and his Indian friends fired a volley of shots into the marching line of British troops. By the time darkness came, the line was reduced to thirty-two soldiers. Two of those were mortally wounded and being carried by their comrades, while three others nursed wounds to arms and legs. Behind them on the road, the wolves followed. Ulrik called Makua to him as the British made camp on the east side of the road.

"Tomorrow these men will join other British soldiers unless we kill them tonight," Ulrik said. "We cannot allow that. I will not allow that. I have made a promise that these men will die. I will call the wolf tonight."

The Indian bowed his head. Ulrik knew the man was afraid. He would not protest, however.

"I will call the wolf," Ulrik repeated. "I want you to take your warriors ahead. Watch the road. Some soldiers may succeed in fleeing. I will trust you to kill them."

"I will do it," Makua said.

"Go then. I will call the wolf when the moon is in the center of the sky."

The Indian slipped away, making the harsh turkey call as he went. His warriors detached themselves from the shadows of trees and followed.

Ulrik waited until full dark. Owls and hawks hunted the night around him. From the north, he could vaguely hear the tearing sounds of the wolves feasting on the slain soldiers. He knew they could smell the fresher blood of the wounded, just as he could.

"Do not gorge yourselves, my friends," Ulrik murmured. "There is much killing still to do."

Ulrik cast another glance toward the campfires of the British. If he strained his ears he could hear the sound of men snoring. He laid his musket aside and quickly pulled off his buckskin clothes. He raised his head and gave the wolf call. Within moments, the alpha male of the pack was at his side, his bushy tail lowered between his hind legs. Naked, Ulrik knelt beside him.

"We have much to do tonight, my brother," he said, taking the animal's head in his hands. "I will need your help."

The wolf blinked his eyes and moaned deep in his chest. Ulrik nodded and released the wolf's head. He took a deep breath and called the other wolf.

He had never known life without the wolf. After nearly one hundred fifty years, it still thrilled his senses to call the wolf, to feel his solid bones melting and reforming, to feel the hair erupting from his flesh, to let the wildness overwhelm him.

His transformation from man to wolf was not complete when the natural wolf he had called pricked up its ears and looked behind Ulrik. The half-man, half-wolf turned and found a big-eyed British soldier staring at him. The man raised a shaking musket to his shoulder and fired.

Ulrik jumped aside, letting the transformation complete itself as he moved. He felt his heart racing within his wolf chest. To be caught in mid-change was deadly; a normal lead musket ball would be enough to kill him at such a moment. He would make the soldier sorry he had ever been born...

He was too late. The natural wolf was already on the man. The soldier fell to the ground under the weight of the animal. His red jacket turned brown around the collar as his throat was torn away.

Ulrik heard more soldiers approaching, alerted by the shot. He raised his head and called the rest of the pack. The howl felt much deeper and fuller coming from his throat now that he wore the shape of the wolf. He didn't wait for an answer, but charged ahead to meet the coming soldiers, the natural wolf following close behind.

They found three redcoats moving quickly through the trees in the direction of the shot. Ulrik sprang on the first man, his jaws fastening on the soldier's neck and snapping it before his teeth even pierced the flesh. The other two men turned to run. The natural wolf jumped on the back of one of them and dragged him to the ground. The soldier screamed and tried to cover his head and neck with his arms as the wolf tore at him. Ulrik ran past, chasing the third man.

All around him, other wolves were rushing forward, toward the British camp. He could hear shots from the camp as the first wolves arrived there. The soldier he was chasing tripped over a root and sprawled on the ground, his musket thrown ahead of him. Ulrik and two other wolves jumped on him, tearing through the cloth of his jacket and trousers, ripping mouthfuls of meat away from his skeleton even as the soldier beat at them with his feeble hands.

Ulrik moved on. Soldiers in various states of dress and wolves with bloody muzzles were running in every direction. Screams and growls filled the darkness. There was an occasional musket shot. Ulrik moved among the melee, killing where he found victims, joining in the feast where other wolves paused to enjoy their prey.

From the south, he heard the rippling crackle of a musket volley and knew some of the soldiers had reached Makua and his warriors. Ulrik left the feast and sped south, calling his pack to join him.

They soon found the bodies of five British soldiers laying on or near the roadway. Ulrik smelled Makua before he saw him. The tall Indian stood with his warriors behind him, watching as the racing wolf pack approached. Makua's eyes were afraid but his face was set. Ulrik raised his head and howled. He raced past Makua without another glance, the pack flowing with him, leaving the Indians behind. Ulrik knew Makua would follow.

There would be killing enough for wolves and Indians alike when they reached Bemis Heights.

Ulrik licked his lips as he ran, tasting the independence of a new nation in the salty fluid drying on his jaws.

# ELYSIA

I was in an office—small, cramped, filled with the trappings of the tiny, withered woman who sat across the desk from me. She was a holy woman in black robes. A silver crucifix hung at her neck, glinting coldly. Her yellowed flesh was stretched tight over fragile bones. Her eyes, sharp and dry, studied me and hated me. She was a keeper of parched, faded secrets—a guardian of the virtue of young girls. Her fear was a sour taste, but I liked it.

"Who are you?" she asked again.

"She knows me," I said.

"Who are you to her?" One skeletal hand fluttered on the desk, wanting to pull the braided gold cord that would summon help. Something within me frightened her. I knew she could be a threat.

I rose from the chair. My dark essence filled the room, shadowy and thick, suffocating the little bird-like woman. Her eyes became as big as moons. Her mouth opened and I could see that she did contain some moisture...

Then I was in a hallway. The tiny, frightened woman was only another tome in my library of sin. I scarcely remember what happened to her. She would not bother me again. The hallway was vast, endless, almost empty. I was an intruder there. I was something masculine, ancient and dark, in a place of virginity and dust. The staccato thunder of my boots sent generations of forgotten dreams and unremembered hopes scurrying for safety. The smell of candles and penance hung as heavy as oil on the air of this hall. The building watched me, reluctantly letting me move within its confines.

At last I found the door. I stood on the threshold but did not enter—this sacrilege I could not do. My eyes picked her out easily enough; she was an inferno of life among a crowd of gray, bent figures who could not see me, could not see their own salvation or damnation.

Our eyes met.

*Elysia...*

She understood my need.

I found myself outside, though still within the inclusive walls of the institution where young girls were educated to their faith. I stood in a courtyard. The late autumn sun was filtered and stained gold and crimson as it fell through the last tenacious leaves of the trees surrounding the yard. I stood on a square dais of smooth gray stone that was as cold as a corpse; the chill rose through my boots and tried to freeze my wicked bones.

I closed my eyes and saw her as she had appeared in my dream. She had been naked, lying on this cold block of stone, her head over the edge so that her red hair fell to the ground like fire from the sky. Her throat, so white and smooth, pulsing under an amber moon, beckoned me with each throb of her life's fluid. After so many years of searching, I knew I had found the one woman who would accept what I offered. My mate, my companion... Elysia. Her name was the dwelling place of happy souls.

When I awoke I knew instinctively where to find her. I traveled with all speed to this fortress of chastity. I found my dear Elysia in the classroom, among other girls who were like coal scattered around a blazing ruby. Would she answer my summons?

She came to stand at the edge of the dais. I offered her my hand and led her to the center of the sharp square.

"If you come away with me, I can promise you pain and disgrace," I said. "But I will love you like no other can."

"Who are you?" she asked, though her eyes told me she knew me as I knew her.

I smiled and circled her, still holding her by the hand, forcing her to turn, to dance with me. I pulled her close and inhaled the fragrance of her hair and flesh. My lips brushed her flushed cheek. Her youth and vitality filled me like a narcotic, intoxicated me.

"Who are you?"

How could I answer? Should I say I am Death? Satan? Surely I came here to steal her innocence, to take the very thing that made up her soul. My lips passed her ear and I whispered what she already knew, "I am Ulrik."

"Yes. I know you," she breathed. "Wolf lord." She tilted her head back to expose her throat, her vulnerability.

My hands fastened on her, one pressing her against me, the other tangled in her thick hair. I let the beast come forward, felt my bones stretching, reshaping themselves into that creature that is neither man nor wolf. With my teeth I tore away the coarse white blouse she wore. I nuzzled the hot, unblemished skin of her bosom before I let my teeth break the flesh of her shoulder. Her blood was wine, was fire, was life on my starving tongue. She tensed, then shuddered in my arms and pressed herself closer to me.

So enraptured was I that I did not sense the holy women of the institution until they were upon us. Hands like the talons of a great bird ripped my lover from my arms. I swooned, still drunk with pleasure at having found what I had so long sought. Slowly I realized the danger. Too late I realized the danger.

Five women, all dressed in heavy, black robes, all wearing silver crucifixes, stood on the dais with me. The one who had torn my Elysia from me was tall, stern, and without fear. She looked at the wound I had made. Elysia swayed before her with closed eyes and a smile on her tender face. I had made her happy. I had made her a woman.

Without hesitation, the holy crone clutched at her crucifix, raised it above her shoulder, and plunged it into the heart of my love. Elysia did not scream. The sweet child sighed and collapsed, lifeless and suddenly cold on the icy stone.

I recovered my senses too late. The woman turned on me, her bloody cross still held in her hand, poised to strike again. Her companions closed around me, also holding their amulets as weapons.

The beast rushed forward, my transformation completed itself, and I stood among them as a huge, savage wolf. Still they did not cower. I could not face death. I did not have the courage to follow my love into the darkness. I broke through the ring of women who held death in their bony hands, leapt over the fence, and fled into the forest.

I ran until my muscles screamed against me and my lungs could not draw breath fast enough to sustain me. I fell to the earth and lay as though dead for many days. Hunger drove me to my feet at last.

I have never found peace, but I found revenge. When the pain of loss dulled, I returned to the holy school and visited the women who had taken my love from me. Their flesh was stale, their blood luke-warm, but I gorged myself. When my revenge was complete, I found the room where my love had slept and left my tears and a white rose on her pillow.

*Elysia...*

# HENRY'S RUN

The sticky, humid forests of northern Mississippi did not like people hurrying through them — especially niggers running away from their rightful owners. Henry waved his arms to clear away clouds of stinging, biting insects and push aside branches that clawed at his clothes and eyes. He knew the trees were trying to hold him, keep him until the slave catchers could find him. His bare feet were bruised and torn from the twisted roots that protruded from the dark soil. He ached. He was afraid, but he kept running.

Not long after noon, he couldn't take it anymore. He had been running for nearly twelve hours. Henry found a space between two mossy boulders and sat down to rest for a moment.

"I'm a-comin,' Beauty," he mumbled. "Daddy's comin' for ya."

His daughter was nine years old. She had been sold a week ago to a man from Arkansas; the man owned a brothel in Little Rock. The light skin Beauty had inherited from her mother had caught the man's attention and he paid a large sum of money for her. Henry had been in the fields when Beauty was taken away in chains.

Tessie, Henry's wife, had gone mad when she saw her daughter taken away. She ran after Beauty's new owner, throwing handfuls of mud and dung at the man. When she was pulled away, she had continued fighting, blinding Master Reynold's son, William, by scratching at his eyes.

Henry had to watch his wife take her beating. She lived for two days after she was cut down from the post.

"You he'p my baby," she had said as Henry washed her the last time. "You gots to he'p my Beauty."

Henry didn't remember falling asleep. When his eyes sprung open he found himself staring into the deep black eyes of a white man. The man was squatting directly in front of Henry, his thick hands dangling between his knees, a serious expression on his bearded face.

"They have the dogs on your trail," the white man said. "Come. We must hurry."

The man's attitude defied argument. Henry got to his sore feet and loped after him. He couldn't hear any dogs, but he knew the slave catchers would use them. Within minutes, his feet were screaming in agony.

An hour later, he heard the dogs. The trees seemed to renew their efforts to hold him for the slave catchers and their dogs.

The white man ahead of him kept moving, only glancing back occasionally to be sure Henry was still following. Henry didn't know if he could trust the man, but he did know the man was taking him in the opposite direction of the dogs. He wondered if the man was one of those people who helped slaves in the Underground Railroad. He'd heard of that. Thinking of it gave him some comfort. He hurried forward to try to talk to the man.

"Dem dogs is gittin' awful close, Massa."

"I am not your master. Keep running. I will take care of the dogs when the time comes for that."

"Yessuh, Mas—" Henry clamped his mouth shut on the word before it was finished. He was a big man, with muscles hardened by a life of manual labor, but this white man had some kind of inner strength that baffled Henry.

"Come. This way. There is a stream not far that will hide our scent. We must get there well ahead of the hounds." The man took Henry by the arm, pulling him forward with a strength the runaway slave could not resist.

"What's yo' name, Mass—"

"Call me Ulrik, if you must call me something," the white man answered. "Hurry."

Henry ducked branches and dodged around thick hardwoods, but couldn't keep from getting scratched, slapped, banged in the shoulders and tripped by thick, dark roots that seemed to reach from the black soil to grab his naked ankles.

Ahead of him, Ulrik moved with the grace of a cat, seeming never to disturb the low-hanging branches or catch his booted feet among the tangled roots. Henry had never seen a white man with such a fluid way of moving.

Behind them, the dogs bayed and barked and howled as if they couldn't wait to find another poor nigger huddled up like a crying baby beside some rock. Henry knew the dogs. He'd seen what they'd done to another runaway. The slave catchers let the dogs play with the tired girl for a while before pulling the animals back. That girl only had one ear now. Scars covered her face, arms and legs. Henry knew he'd been a fool to think he could outrun the dogs.

"Do not listen to them," Ulrik said, pausing for a moment. Henry stopped beside him, panting and wiping stinging sweat from his eyes. "The dogs are nothing to us. I can take care of the dogs. We must draw them ahead of the men, though. Come now." He was off again, slipping between the trees like a ghost. The whooping of the slave catchers was barely audible behind the voices of the hounds. Henry took a deep breath and charged after the white man.

He had heard of the man named Josef Ulrik. The big white man had been a plantation owner himself, but his neighbors in Louisiana burned his house and crop because Ulrik let his slaves buy their freedom with their labor. Since then, he had become a helper to slaves who ran away. But a slave on the run couldn't count on Ulrik being nearby—no more than he could count on being safe in Ulrik's company.

Messages from slaves who had successfully escaped some- times trickled back to the Deep South. Some told of being helped by Ulrik, a strong, fierce white man who could get away from hounds and men with the skill of a deadly angel. Once, however, a slave was found mutilated and babbling, but alive. He told of meeting the white man named Ulrik. He called the man a devil, an eater of men. That slave died before his wounds healed; a wolf came into the slave quarters and killed him. Many said Ulrik sent the wolf, that he controlled wolves and rats and other mean- spirited animals. Slave owners encouraged the story of a cannibal living in the forests of the South to keep their slaves obedient.

"You ain't gonna kill me, is ya Massa Ulrik?" Henry asked.

"It is no wish of mine," Ulrik answered. "We are nearly to the water, and the dogs have drawn ahead of the hunters. Do not delay."

"Yessuh." Henry tried to make his legs pump faster, but couldn't get any more speed from his tired limbs. He crashed into the trunk of an elm and staggered back. Ulrik grabbed his arms and pulled him forward. Within minutes they were on the bank of a wide, shallow creek. Henry fell to his knees and plunged his face under the swift, cold water.

"Enough." Ulrik pulled Henry's face out of the water and dragged him to his feet. "That way is north. Go now. Stay in the center of the stream. It is shallow for many miles in this season. I will join you again very soon. Go!" He pushed Henry into the water and turned away.

The cold water and soft, cool mud of the creek bed felt good on Henry's sore feet. He watched as Ulrik slipped back into the forest, toward the sound of the approaching dogs. For a moment, Henry thought he saw the white man pulling his shirt off as he ran. Henry turned away and splashed to the middle of the creek. He turned north, but froze where he stood as a new sound filled the woods.

It was an animal sound, but not like any animal Henry had ever heard. The long, savage howl ended in something akin to the laughter of a man touched by the Devil. The baying of the dogs changed. Henry could hear them growling and barking. The sound of the fight made the woods seem darker, more sinister. Henry suddenly didn't like being alone.

Beauty waited somewhere up North, waited for her Daddy to save her from the hungry embraces of paying white men. Henry knew he would need help to find her. Ulrik could provide that help. But Ulrik had gone back to face the dogs and the thing that made the other animal noise. Ulrik might need his help. Henry left the water and went back the way he had come.

He found the dogs. There had been ten of them. Pieces of the hounds were scattered among the trees not far from the creek. The fighting sounds had lessened as the number of dogs diminished. Only three were left, backed against a rock, facing a gray and black wolf that was nearly half as tall as Henry. Ulrik was nowhere to be seen. Henry cowered behind a thick oak.

The wolf turned and faced him for a moment. Henry knew the black eyes. They were human eyes. Ulrik's eyes.

The three dogs rushed the wolf as its attention was on the man. Henry could hear the shouts of hunters as they ran toward the fight. He turned away and ran back to the water, crossing the stream and running through the woods as fast as he could, his earlier weariness forgotten.

The sound of fighting animals died behind him. Henry kept running. He barely noticed the gnarled roots or groping branches as he ran. He wouldn't look behind him.

When the wolf appeared at his side, Henry felt his bowels loosen and for a moment he thought he would mess his pants as he ran. With a flick of its massive head, the wolf caught Henry's shirt and flung him to the ground. Henry rolled over and over and finally bumped to a stop, the knuckles of tree roots digging into his back.

Ulrik stood over him, a naked white man with sad but vicious eyes.

"It was very unwise of you to follow me," Ulrik said. "My secret cannot be known. You understand that."

It wasn't a question, but Henry nodded vigorously. "Yessuh, Massa, I unnerstand that. Yessuh."

Ulrik nodded too, slowly and without breaking eye contact. "I am sorry. Truly I am."

The man's shape melted and reformed as Henry gaped, motionless against the trunk of the tree. He didn't think to scream until the wolf's teeth closed on his throat. There was a moment of pain. He could feel his blood, hot and sticky, running down his chest, coloring his ragged shirt and mixing with his sweat.

Henry could hear his heart beating.

*thum THUMP thum THUMP*

He could hear Ulrik pulling and chewing at his flesh. The world darkened. All sound, except the beating of his heart, faded away. Henry relaxed.

*thum THUMP thum THUMP*

Like bare feet running on a well-worn path to a better place.

A new light appeared. Henry saw Tessie in the light. The whip marks were gone. Her flesh was smooth and unblemished. She held her arms out to him.

"You did the best ya could, Henry," Tessie said.

*thum THUMP thum THUMP*

"I will find your daughter." Ulrik's voice was a blaring intrusion in the world of light. "She will be safe."

"She a good girl," Henry said, a red bubble exploding from his mouth with his last words.

*thum THUMP thum THUMP*

He found freedom in the darkness.

# CALL TO THE HUNT

Snow was falling softly outside. It was a welcome change from the blowing blizzard that had raged for the past three days and nights. The storm was over; the snow falling now was almost like a whispered apology for the fury that came before.

Inside a small log cabin high in the Black Hills of the Dakota Territory, Josef Ulrik sat near a pot-bellied stove, his hands extended toward the warmth of the stove's open door. Snow melted and dripped from his thick beard, matting the hair so the new gray highlights were slicked against the dark hair of his youth. Except for the heavy blanket draped over his shoulders, he was naked. A dead white rabbit lay on the floor beside him, a droplet of blood occasionally falling from the wound on its neck.

When his hands were warm, Ulrik picked up the rabbit by the ears and flopped its limp body onto a rough-hewn table in one corner of the cabin's single room. He plucked a knife from a shelf over the table and deftly peeled away the white fur. He tossed the skin toward the door of the cabin, then sliced the rabbit into pieces. He placed an iron skillet on the top of the stove, added a glob of lard, and dropped the pieces of rabbit into the skillet. Soon the cabin was filled with the smell and sound of sizzling meat.

Ulrik absently pushed the pieces of meat around in the skillet to keep them from sticking. He plucked light, loose hair from his arms and brushed more from his naked torso. He was thinking of how nice it would be to have a hot, cooked meal and considering adding potatoes to his dinner menu when he heard a sound outside his cabin. He pulled on his trousers and grabbed his rifle, then threw the blanket around his shoulders again as the sound neared his front door.

Footsteps. Two sets of them crunching through the snow. Now one hurried away. Ulrik threw the door open, his carbine held loosely in his right hand. An Indian girl stood meekly on his small porch, her head down. An older man was running away.

"Stop!" Ulrik commanded. The Indian turned to look, but kept running. Ulrik fired a shot over the fleeing man's shoulder. "I said 'Stop'," he called. The Indian stopped running. He waited a long moment before turning around. "Come here." The Indian trudged through the snow back toward the cabin until he was standing on the porch beside the girl.

"Who are you?" Ulrik asked.

"I am called Dark Feather," the Indian answered. He was Sioux, Ulrik noted, dressed in leather pants and shirt with a coat of moose hide hanging from his shoulders to his knees. Except for a knife at his waist, he was unarmed.

"Why do you come here? Why do you leave this girl at my door?"

The Indian kept his head high, but his face showed internal pain as he answered. "She is my daughter. She—she is no longer welcome in our village. She has been touched by the wolf spirit."

"Explain what you mean," Ulrik said.

The man took his daughter's head in his hands, gently but firmly, and tilted her face back. He spread her lips so that Ulrik could see her teeth. One of her incisors was broken off. When Dark Feather saw that Ulrik noted this, he released his daughter. She lowered her head again.

"Her name is Kiona," Dark Feather said. "She is called Broken Tooth now. She runs with the wolves. She sings with the wolves. She broke her tooth eating a buffalo killed by the wolves. She was sharing in their kill." He looked at Ulrik as if he expected the white man to say his daughter was crazy.

"Why do you bring her to me?" Ulrik asked.

"Because you, too, sing with the wolves. You know them even better than my daughter. She cannot return to our people. I would not leave her to die in the forest," the Sioux finished quietly. "I have no other children."

Ulrik looked at the child. She was a slender thing, dressed much like her father, though she wore a leather skirt instead of pants. Rabbit fur was tied around her shins. Her moccasins were wet. Her bare hands trembled at her sides.

"I do not take her as a wife," Ulrik said. "I will take her as a daughter and teach her that which she needs to know. She will be safe here."

"I will come to see her. I—"

"No. You will not see her," Ulrik said. "She is dead to you, and you to her. To have it otherwise would cause her to return to your village. Your people will not allow that. She will be well. You have my promise."

The Indian stared at Ulrik for a moment, his face set, then he turned on his heel and trotted away through the snow. He did not look back at his daughter or the white man he left her with. Not that Ulrik saw. Once the Sioux disappeared into the tree line, Ulrik heard the warrior raise a cry of despair. He knew the Indian would tell his people he had killed his strange daughter.

"Come inside, child," Ulrik said. He could smell his supper burning behind him. Reluctantly, the girl obeyed. Ulrik closed the door. "Sit down and I will bring you some hot food." He pointed toward the table and the single chair before it. The girl sat mutely, her head still bowed.

They ate in silence. The girl kept her eyes on her tin plate, tearing her meat with her fingers and chewing quickly. When she was finished, she put her hands in her lap and continued to stare at her empty plate.

"Do you think you are a wolf?" Ulrik asked at last. The girl nodded, paused, and shook her head. "Which is it? Yes or no?" She finally raised her eyes to look at him.

"I think that my spirit leaves my body and becomes a wolf," she said. "I thought it was dreams. My father says that I sing the wolf song in my sleep.

"One day I was gathering wood for our fire and I saw the wolves and they saw me and they came to me and were around me and I ran with them as I am. They accepted me. Since then, they have come close to our village and called to me. I go to them. I hunt with them."

"Have you been bitten by a wolf, child?"

"No."

"This is strange," Ulrik said. "I have not heard of this before. Did any of these wolves ever change its shape and become a man or woman?"

Her eyes showed her confusion. She shook her head. "No," she said. "Is it true that you have that power? My people say you were once a wolf and the coyote tricked you into becoming a man. You are only allowed to return to your wolf skin when the moon is full."

"I have always been a man," Ulrik answered. "But I have also been a wolf for all of the life I can remember. It is true that I can change from man to wolf and back again. I do so at will, but when the moon is full, I am the wolf only."

"You will give this gift to me?" Her face was eager. She placed her palms on the top of the table and leaned forward.

Ulrik studied her for a long moment. At last he nodded once.

"It is said that the Pack will gather," he said. "When that happens, there can be no culls among us—no weaklings. There will be one among us who can produce our kind naturally, without violence. Perhaps…"

"You think I am that one?"

"I do not know," Ulrik said, shaking his head. "It is not natural, the things you say you have done. The things you say you can do. Perhaps you are the one. Have you had the blood yet?"

She looked at him, puzzled.

"The blood that makes you a woman," he said.

"No."

Ulrik nodded slowly.

"Will you give me the gift now?"

"No. Not now. I must think first. I must know. The freedom to release the beast within is not something to be given lightly. Go to sleep now." He waved one thick hand toward the narrow bed in another corner of the cabin.

The girl looked at the bed and back at him warily.

"Sleep child." Ulrik smiled. "I will sit here and think and when I am ready I will sleep on the floor."

The girl went to the bed and soon Ulrik heard her breathing deeply and steadily. He remained at the table, waiting. Soon he heard the howl of a wolf. It was answered by another. Then a chorus took up the song. It was a call to the hunt. The girl stirred restlessly in the bed. Ulrik watched her.

Kiona clawed the blankets off her body and writhed on the thin mattress stuffed with autumn grass. She bared her teeth and licked her lips. Finally she arched her back and answered the call, her thin, high voice filling the cabin. She sprang from the bed and ran for the door. Ulrik caught her and held her in his arms, pressing her close as she struggled against him. Her eyes were savage blanks, her face an angry snarl. She snapped at him, saliva spraying his face as he dodged her mouth.

With a great effort, Ulrik got a heavy blanket around the girl. He rolled her in it, pinning her arms tightly to her sides, then bound the blanket with a piece of rope. He lifted her from the floor and put her back on the bed. She thrashed against her binding, her face still contorted with rage, pausing only occasionally to throw her head back and answer the wolves who had moved closer to the cabin.

Near dawn, the wolves outside gave up and moved away. Slowly, the girl in the bed settled back into a peaceful sleep, her eyes closing and her limbs relaxing. Ulrik touched her soft face, moved a lock of her long black hair off her sweaty brow. He spread a blanket on the floor and slept until the sun was high in the sky.

When he awoke, he was greeted by the solemn, steady gaze of the Sioux girl. She lay where he had left her, still bound in the blanket. Ulrik got to his feet, stiff from the hours spent on the hard dirt floor.

"Good morning, Kiona Brokentooth," he said.

"Why am I tied like this?"

"You do not remember anything from the night?"

"No. Did I have the wolf dream again?"

"You did. I bound you to keep you from going to them."

"Why?"

"They are pure animals, without reason," Ulrik said. "That you do not remember trying to go to them makes me believe you would become like them in mind as well as body. You are not the one I spoke of last night. You are not the Mother of the Pack."

"But you will still give me your gift."

Ulrik didn't answer. He only looked at the girl and watched the hope die in her black eyes.

"Untie me, please," she said. "I must make water."

Ulrik untied her and helped her out of the bed. He watched her leave the cabin, then went to the shelf over the table and took some pieces of dried venison from a bag there. He tried to ignore the disappointment he felt. He knew in his heart the time was not right for the Mother of the Pack to emerge. Still, he felt it was his destiny to find the one.

He dropped the uneaten meat onto the table and pulled off his clothes. He closed his eyes and called the wolf. Within moments, the thick-chested man had changed his shape to that of a large black wolf. He bounded through the door after the Indian girl.

Ulrik found her squatted over a bowl she'd carved in the snow behind the cabin. She showed no surprise when he trotted up to her. She finished urinating, a fast hard stream of pungent fluid, then stood up, letting her buckskin skirt fall past her knees. She stepped away from the puddle she had made, toward the wolf. His head was on a level with her chest. She raised a hand and stroked the area between his ears.

Ulrik knew if he thought about what he was doing he would stop himself. He didn't want to stop. She was young, but she obviously had some gift already. There was something special about the child. No one could deny that she was meant to receive the Gift.

He had been too long without another of his own kind for company. Kiona Brokentooth was only a child, but she knew the beast and would welcome his kiss.

Ulrik pushed his muzzle into her chest, tearing open her shirt with his teeth and finding the smooth young flesh beneath. He nipped her, just enough to bring the blood. He licked the wound roughly, forcing the child to put both hands around his neck just to remain on her feet. It was enough, he knew. It took very little of the wolf's saliva to pass the Gift to another.

He smelled them as they drew near. From all around, the wolves came to witness the passing of the Gift to this child. They raised their voices, dozens of them, and sang to the afternoon sun.

Even as Ulrik lapped the blood from her bosom, the girl threw back her head and howled with the wolves.

Then she pushed Ulrik away and tore blindly at her clothes until she stood naked before him. Astonished and wary, Ulrik watched the child change shape as if she had been born with the ability. Soft black hair sprouted from the pores of her flesh, a tail erupted from her backside, her fingers drew into her palms while the hands themselves thickened into the paws of a beast. She dropped to all fours, her face a picture of childish ecstasy. Her mouth opened and he saw that her canines had already grown long and sharp; the broken incisor remained damaged, but Ulrik knew it would not hinder her ability to rend flesh.

At last she was done. Kiona Brokentooth stood before him, an eager young wolf ready for her first hunt. All around them, the natural wolves welcomed her, calling her to join them. Ulrik raised his own head and joined the song. Kiona sang with him.

She has much to learn, Ulrik thought. He would keep her close and perhaps in time he would learn what her destiny was.

For now, however, there was only the snow and the wind and the song of the wolves calling them to the hunt.

# LATENT LYCANTHROPY

The girl stood out like a ballerina in a morgue. Third row, fourth desk back. She wore a breezy white dress covered in pastel butterflies, short white socks with lace ruffles, and shiny black shoes. She was hunched over her desk. Mike Rupe could see that she had her knees pressed together so hard the bones must be rubbing.

*If she needs something, she'll have to raise her hand.*

He glanced her way again and saw that she was chewing her lower lip. Her feet were raised so only her toes touched the floor; she bounced her feet nervously.

"Does everyone have this book out?" Mike realized several minutes had passed since he showed his first grade class the spelling book and told them to take it from their desks. Several children blinked at him.

*What is her name?* His seating chart was already buried under other papers. *Damn expensive college can't teach a person how to be organized.*

"Okay, open your books to page one." He held his book up for all to see again. "There's a big picture of a red apple on the page. Does everyone have it? Good."

The girl's deep brown eyes darted around the classroom as though checking to see if any of the other first graders were watching her. A long, thick lock of hair so black it was almost blue fell into her face. The girl didn't dare unfold her small hands to brush it away. She blew at it once, but it didn't move. Her eyes flitted around the room again, as if afraid someone would hear the hiss of her breath.

*What is it with her?*

Mike put his spelling book aside and dug through the papers on his desk until he found the seating chart.

"Shara," he called. "Shara Wellington? Is something wrong?"

She was bent over her desk so that her chin nearly rested on the open book. She tried to straighten herself, but couldn't. It looked like she was having cramps. Her face puckered.

"Shara? What is it?" Mike jumped from his chair and started around his desk.

"I have to go to the bathroom," the girl answered in a husky whisper. "Real bad." Her eyes flickered over the classroom again. Now everyone was looking at her.

"Okay." Mike stopped. *Thank God she's not sick.* He tried to smile at her. "You can go ahead."

Slowly, the girl swung her legs around and stood up from her desk, her knees still clamped together. She was distinctly, painfully aware of the other students watching her. The butterfly dress clung to her buttocks. Mike could see that she knew this and was too embarrassed to reach around and pull it loose. She took a step forward, then froze. A tear loosed itself from one dark eye and ran down her cheek. She hung her head.

"Look at that!" a skinny, blond, freckle-faced boy bellowed. *Richard Tibbs.* The boy pointed at Shara's feet. "She peed on the floor."

The classroom exploded with laughter. More tears ran down Shara's face. She sobbed. The puddle at her feet grew. She wanted to run; Mike could read it in her mortified expression. He could remember that feeling. Mike pictured himself sitting in a closet of his childhood home, too ashamed to come out for dinner. *I know what you're feeling, little girl. I know.*

"Be quiet!" His voice silenced the room. *It's good to be the king.*

Mike smiled for the deep, pain-filled eyes that rolled up to meet him as he hurried up the aisle. He scooped Shara off the floor and carried her out of the classroom, ignoring the warm wetness of her dress. She pushed her face into his shoulder and dampened his shirt with her tears. Mike wanted to hug her and give her the comforting words he had wished for on that long ago day he spent in his closet. He put her on her feet in the hallway before the girl's restroom and pushed the door open.

"Go on, Shara, it's all right," he urged. He pushed gently on her back. She moved forward on shuffling feet. Mike let the door close behind her.

He stood outside the door of the girl's restroom and remembered with perfect clarity a long ago day when he had left school early and raced home, hoping to arrive unnoticed. Hoping he could be clean before his mother returned home from her afternoon grocery shopping. Hoping the school wouldn't notice the absence of one little boy. No such luck.

The restroom door opened and Shara came out slowly, her head down so that she watched her shuffling black shoes. She stopped in front of the teacher but didn't look up at him. Mike looked down at her dark head, at the part of her hair, and smiled. He squatted before her and tilted her head back so she had to meet his eyes.

"Feel better?" he asked.

"Yes." Her voice was a whisper. "I'm wet."

"Yeah. You are." Mike smiled at her again. "You'll need to go home and change your clothes."

"My mom will be mad at me."

"Why didn't you tell me earlier that you needed to go?"

"Because we already had our bathroom break," Shara said. "But… I couldn't go then. They wouldn't let me close the door. I didn't want them to watch."

"Ah. I see," Mike said, nodding. "And you thought I wouldn't let you go?"

She nodded.

"And maybe you thought everyone would laugh at you if you asked to go and I said no?"

Again, she nodded.

"What happened?"

"I peed in class."

Mike couldn't help but chuckle. "Well, yes, but I meant that you ended up with everybody looking at you anyway. It would have been better if you'd just asked to go when you needed to, wouldn't it?"

"Yes."

"Don't be afraid to speak up in class. Okay, Shara?"

"Okay."

"The school day's about over, so let's go call your mom and let you go home early."

"Okay."

"You know you're not the first person to have an accident in first grade, right?"

She only looked at him with her large dark eyes without making any answer.

"It happens to a lot of people. Some of them even go on to become teachers. Like me."

Realization dawned in her eyes like a faraway lamp that grew brighter and brighter. Finally, the light touched her lips and she smiled. Mike led her to the office and called her mother, then returned to a classroom that had become unruly in his absence.

* * *

The show-and-tell session ended. Mike Rupe lined his pupils in a row and led them out for recess. He didn't notice the dark-haired girl who remained behind. When Shara came to the playground late he watched as she ignored her classmates and came to stand before him. A bit of red fuzz clung to her chin; her eyes were wide and bright.

"I'm sick. I need to go home," she announced.

"What's wrong?" Mike asked.

"My stomach."

"What's wrong with it?" Since the episode where she'd urinated in class, Mike had caught Shara returning an occasional smile in class. He didn't think she'd lie to him just to go home. "Is your stomach cramping, or do you feel like you need to throw up?"

"Both. Real bad." The fleck of red fuzz twitched in the light breeze.

"Both, huh? Maybe you'd feel better if you just went to the office and lay down for a while." The teacher reached out and flicked the piece of fuzz from the girl's chin.

"No, Mr. Rupe. I need to go home. I feel really bad."

Mike sighed and looked up, surveyed the playground of children, and gave in. "Okay, Shara. Let's go call your mom."

Mike waited as Maria Costello, the school secretary called Shara's mom. When it was confirmed Shara had a ride home, he told her to take care of herself and returned to the playground, where recess was just about over. He corralled the rest of his students and led them inside, shushing them as they passed rooms where class was still in session, finally waving them into their own classroom.

Richard Tibbs ran to his desk and grabbed the stuffed parrot he had brought for show-and-tell. It was a toy his father had brought home from Mexico one month before he died in a military training accident at the local air force base. "Somebody tore it!" he screamed.

Shocked, Mike could only stand for a moment and look at the class bully standing beside his desk, holding the mauled toy and sobbing. Then he recovered and went to Richard, gently taking the toy from his hands.

The bright red breast of the bird was torn open. Bits of cotton spilled from the bird's body. Hesitantly, Mike touched the wound. It was damp around the edges. *Saliva?*

Mike remembered Richard leading the class in teasing Shara when she urinated on the floor.

*Shara had red fuzz on her chin when she left.* He looked again at the ragged wound on the toy's breast. *I brushed it off her.*

# Biological Clock

"No, you can't come in," Shara said, her voice almost a plea. "You can't."

"Shara, this has gone far enough." Bryan McWaters pushed on the attic door, but not as hard as he could; Shara knew he still worried he would hurt her. She pushed back, determined to keep the barrier between her and her husband. "Come on, Shara. I gave in when you refused to go to a doctor, and I called the midwife back and told her we didn't need her, but, dammit, I'm coming in there."

"No!" Suddenly Shara pushed with all her might and forced the door completely closed. She threw the first bolt, then more slowly drew the last three into place. On the other side, her husband implored, then pounded, kicked, and finally cursed, but Shara did not open the door.

Another pain ripped through her body and Shara doubled over, her hands clutching her swollen abdomen. A short, sharp cry escaped her clenched lips. Bryan stopped cussing.

"Shara, please," he begged.

"No," she gasped. Thick black hair hung in her face and sweat dripped from her nose. Bryan had said he loved the feel and color of her hair once. *Will he ever say it again?* "There's things I didn't tell you, Bryan. I'm older than you think. I'll be all right. And—" Another labor pain sent her to her knees. "And when it's over, we'll have to talk. Now go. I'll call you when it's over. I'll tell you when the baby's here."

"I'm not going anywhere," Bryan answered stubbornly. Had she startled him? Shara was in too much pain to tell.

She got to her feet and staggered across the small attic room she had been secretly preparing for the past few months. Slowly, she lowered herself onto the soft pallet of quilts. The pains came close and hard now. She struggled from her clothes and lay on her back, waiting.

*Poor Bryan. Maybe I should have told him everything right from the beginning.*

"I told you my monthlies were hell," she mumbled. Her mind drifted back to the early days of their relationship while her hands rested on her belly, feeling the lives within as they prepared to emerge into the world.

The problem hadn't been so bad when they were dating. Her monthly, or period, or cycle, or whatever, only lasted three days. It could have been worse; she knew of others who went a full week and sometimes more. She wouldn't let Bryan anywhere around her when her monthly came. When it was time, she would make some excuse and run away, to the mountains or the forests of western Oregon.

Bryan had learned to tolerate it, though he never liked it. Shara had taken it as a sign he really loved her. Why else would a man want to be around his woman while she was on her period? *If my monthlies only consisted of blood, cramps and a short temper...*

Then they had married, and Bryan had been more reluctant to allow her to leave him when her time came. She had always found a way to get out of the house—out of the area where her husband could be in danger. Often she escaped only after a bitter argument, but she endured that, thinking only of what the consequences might be if she remained. When she returned, he would sulk, but they would eventually make up their differences. At least for a month.

Then the monthlies stopped coming, and Shara knew she was pregnant. At first, she hadn't known what to do. They weren't ready for children. Bryan didn't know enough about her. She had considered abortion, but her motherly instincts wouldn't allow it. And besides, the doctor would have learned her secret.

Bryan had discovered her pregnancy, as she knew he must, and he was thrilled. *Will he be so happy when this day is over?*

"They're not yours," Shara sobbed, her hands balled into fists and pushing on the hard floor under the quilts. She tightened her muscles, straining to eject the new life from her body. One tiny lump left her and she let herself relax, waiting for the next pain and the next of her offspring. She didn't look at the first, not yet.

These children weren't Bryan's. Shara was sure of that. *I have to be very in tune with my biological clock.* She hadn't told Bryan. *If it had been just another man, then maybe I could have told him. But how could I tell him this?* He would see for himself soon enough.

Shara screamed as the second child squeezed from her loins, followed immediately by the third. Then it was finished. She lay still, exhausted and sweating, listening to their tiny, confused cries. Slowly, painfully, Shara curled her body around those of her children. They were beautiful, she thought, so like their father. She touched them, stroked them, whispered motherly words to them. Two sons and a daughter. Shara smiled.

She began cleaning her babies. The taste was like nectar to her elated tongue. She pulled them close to let them nurse, idly wishing for a third breast, and then she slept.

Shara awoke an hour later. Bryan was knocking on the door again. He was begging to be let in. He sounded near tears. Shara checked her children and saw that they were asleep. She rose and hurried to the door.

"Just a minute," she called out softly. "They're asleep. Let me get cleaned up." Bryan was quiet. Shara hurried to the wash basin she had prepared and quickly scrubbed the dried blood and after-birth from her thighs, crotch, and breasts, then dressed in a long, loose gown of white satin. She went to the door and released the bolts that held it closed.

Bryan rushed into the room, glanced hurriedly at her, then turned his attention to the pallet on the floor, to the babies lying there in peaceful slumber. He seemed suddenly frozen. Shara moved behind him and put a hand on his shoulder.

"I have to tell you something," she whispered. "First, they'll learn to control their shapes. The teeth, the contours of the head, even the hair, it can be shed and re-grown at will once they learn control. Except during their monthlies. They'll have to give in to their other half then. Now you understand why I go away once a month."

Bryan remained statue-still.

"I'm sorry, Bryan," Shara offered. "It was during my last period. I was in the mountains, and I was running with a pack. The alpha male wanted me, and who was I, a stray bitch with a strange scent, to refuse the leader? It was wrong of me, I know, and I regretted letting it happen. But, Bryan, they're still half me. Isn't that good enough?"

"They're *animals*." His voice was low, choked, scared. He finally turned his eyes back to her. "What the hell are you? Why me?" He turned and ran from the room.

Shara slumped to the floor, crying. She had loved her husband so much until this very moment. And now... She knew it was over. She could hear him moving around in the room below her. He was in the closet. Was he packing? His own clothes, or hers? Then Shara heard a sharp, familiar noise that brought her head up and stopped her tears.

Bryan was coming back up the stairs, and he was running.

Shara sprang to her feet and rushed at the door, trying to close it and get the bolts into place before Bryan got to the top of the steps. She didn't make it. The door burst open and Shara slammed into the wall. She sank to the floor, barely aware of the scream rising in her throat.

Bryan stood in the doorway, his shotgun in his hands, his eyes fixed on the squirming pups; they were awake now and crying for food. Shara watched him raise the gun. She felt her hands thicken and her jaw stretch.

A roar filled the room and Bryan turned to face her. The transformation was only half complete and Shara knew she was terribly vulnerable at this time, but her husband had to be stopped. She was still the size of a woman. She still stood on her hind legs. Her body itched as thick, glossy black hair sprouted from every pore. She saw the fear in Bryan's eyes, and it enraged her.

The white satin robe billowed like a banner as Shara pounced. She grabbed the shotgun with hands that were neither human nor canine. Bryan tried to pull the weapon away from her. They moved as if dancing for a moment. Their faces nearly touched and Shara could scent the terror coming from the man in sickening waves.

Shara only wanted to take the shotgun away from him. Bryan wouldn't let go. The gun twisted around, Bryan's finger caught in the trigger guard. The babies were frightened and calling for her. Shara jerked on the gun. The room filled with thunder and the smell of smoke and fresh blood.

Bryan staggered away from her, his hands now free of the gun, his stomach splattered on the wall behind him. He turned surprised, pain-filled eyes on her, then fell dead at Shara's feet.

Shara dropped the gun and returned to her children. Her shape shifted and she was once again a woman, the widow of the man on the floor. She gathered her whimpering offspring into her arms and stepped over Bryan's corpse, pausing in the doorway.

"We'll go back to the mountains," she whispered to her young. "I'll teach you everything you need to know. Maybe we'll find Ulrik. We may need him." She sighed. "We'll have a good life." Then she looked at the body of her husband.

"I'm sorry, Bryan," she said. "I should have told you everything right from the start. I'll always try to think of you for what you were, and not what you became. It's partly my fault. Maybe you wouldn't have reacted that way if I had told you... everything." A last tear fell from her eye onto the head of one of the pups. "Good-bye."

Shara closed the door on her husband and the short life they had shared.

# Show Me

"Show me."

"No."

"Show me." The little girl pleaded with her sweet mouth and big, soft blue eyes. The shadow of a bruise still darkened her jaw below the left ear. An Oreo cookie crumb clung to one corner of her mouth. Her small pink tongue darted out, swished across the bottom lip and drew the crumb inside.

"No." The old man smiled and shook his head. "I would scare you."

"I don't believe you." She pouted.

Josef Ulrik's smile grew wider. "You would say your grandmother is a liar, then?"

The girl, Dora, hesitated. "No. But maybe she's wrong."

"Maybe. Have another cookie." Ulrik held the package of Double Stuffs toward her. The neighbor child took two more. Such a thin arm, the man thought. *And the dress she wears. It is thin and frayed. If her mother would spend money on clothes for her child rather than alcohol and illicit drugs for herself, the child could be more beautiful than she already is.*

"What is your mother doing today?" he asked.

"Sleeping," Dora answered.

"And your grandmother?"

"Sleeping," the child said. "Gramma was awake all night. She was coughing. She says it's the New Orleans humidity. She doesn't like America. She wants to go back to Germany. She said she wants to die where Grampa died."

Ulrik nodded.

"And she said you have to be a werewolf because your eyebrows grow together over your nose," Dora added.

"She is right," Ulrik said and smiled again. He was sure the child had eaten no breakfast. He should give her something more than cookies. *She should have meat. Fresh meat.*

"Show me," she begged. "I won't be scared."

"How old is your grandmother?"

"Eighty-six. How old are you?"

Ulrik laughed. "I am older. Far, far older. Werewolves live a long, long time."

"You could marry my Gramma," the child suggested. "Then maybe she wouldn't talk about Grampa all the time. Would you be good to her and feed her her oatmeal like I do? I could still come over and do it, if you wanted."

"Ah, child, do you think your grandmother would marry a werewolf?"

"I don't think you are a werewolf. You won't show me."

Such thin legs, Ulrik thought. *Like twigs. And dirty bare feet. How long since anyone had cared enough to make the child bathe?*

"Is there no one to take care of your grandmother in Germany" Ulrik asked.

"No. Momma is her only relative. She wants to go home to die."

"Getting old is not pleasant," Ulrik said quietly.

"How old are you, really?" Dora asked.

Ulrik looked at the girl. He saw her blue eyes, her unwashed blonde hair and her pure innocence. He remembered another girl from his own past — a dark-haired girl with dark eyes like pools of deep thought. That girl had a child now. A boy child with a great destiny. He would need a companion. A mate. Perhaps…

"I am nearly four hundred years old, my cub," Ulrik said. He watched the girl's eyes widen in disbelief. "Yes, child, werewolves live to be very old, indeed. I am old now, even for a werewolf. My joints become stiff when the weather turns cold and I do not like to be alone."

"Show me." She whispered the request.

"It is a great thing to become the wolf," Ulrik continued. "The wolf does not grow old. The wolf is always young and strong."

The old man watched the child's face as he let his beard grow fuller, thicker and darker. He showed her a hand, letting the fingers draw back toward the thickening palm while hair burst from the flesh. Her eyes moved up his arm and back to his face.

"She was right?"

"Yes, child, your grandmother told you true."

"Show me more."

"Are you hungry, my cub?"

The girl nodded.

"You would like to have meat?"

She nodded again.

"I can show you how to have fresh meat. You will never need to be hungry again. I will take you to a place I know where you can learn the ways of the wolf. You would like that?"

"Momma? And Gramma?"

Ulrik put a reassuring, deformed hand on the child's shoulder. "They will not miss you, my cub. You are a burden to them. I can give you what they never will."

"Show me."

"Yes, my cub, I will show you."

The old man let the wolf come forward. The years slipped away and his bones stretched and reformed themselves into the shape of the beast. He raised his head, his nose, toward the ceiling of the moldering house where he had lived for the past three months. The squalor of this temporary dwelling disgusted him suddenly.

As a wolf, he stood as tall as the child of seven years. He looked into her eyes and saw no fear.

"Mr. Ulrik," she whispered. "It really is true." She threw her arms around his neck and hugged him, burying her face in the thick fur of his throat.

Ulrik let his teeth slip through the ragged cotton of the dress. He hesitated only a moment at the smooth, young flesh of the shoulder, then pinched the skin between his teeth and tasted the hot, vital blood. The girl gasped, then snuggled closer, not unused to the pain associated with love.

# SUNDAY DENTISTRY

Jarrod Golding woke slowly. The phone was ringing. It rang and rang and rang and wouldn't stop. It hurt his head. *Too many martinis. Too many beers.* And he was alone in his bed. *Dear God, my life is like a bad country and western song.*

"Hello." His voice was thick and yeasty. The red lights of the digital clock said the time was 7:13 a.m. Yesterday was Saturday. The party was Saturday night. It had to be Sunday morning. Now it was 7:14 a.m.

"Dr. Golding?"

"Yeah."

"I have an appointment scheduled for you at nine o'clock." Female voice, young, pretty. It belonged to a middle-aged fat lady—his answering service operator.

"Today?"

"Yes, Doctor." The pretty tone vanished. "That's more than the thirty-minute notice you required."

"Yeah, yeah, it is," Jarrod admitted. He felt as if his head was expanding like a balloon. He wondered when the clown would twist him into an animal shape. "Listen, will you call Katie for me? Ask her to meet me at the office."

"Yes, Doctor, I can do that." The woman's tone was sweet again.

"Who's the patient?"

"Robert Tate. A new patient. He says he broke a tooth on a steak bone."

"New patient. Great. Thanks." Jarrod hung up the phone and rolled over in bed. He pulled the covers over his head, then threw them off. If he was going to have any coffee, he had to get the machine going now.

The cold shower was like a slap in the face from God, but Jarrod felt much better when it was over. The smell of the coffee was filling the house. Life wasn't so bad after all, he admitted before he burned his tongue on the black liquid. He sipped slowly and chewed delicately at a piece of light toast, his stomach not making too much of a protest over the food.

At the age of twenty-seven, he knew he was really too young to have his own dentistry practice. He should be officed with an old saw who was already established. He could wait the old man out, then take over a steady practice. But, when Jarrod's parents had died in an auto accident during his last year of residency, he'd decided to use the inheritance to skip ahead and open his own office in the small town of Windy Acres, Oklahoma. He was the only dentist in town; everyone had been forced to make the drive to Enid to have their teeth worked on until three months ago. Enid had good dentists, and several bars that made decent martinis.

Making his services available for emergencies had been Jarrod's idea, too. He'd wanted to establish goodwill with the people of his new home. As the hands of the kitchen clock reached for 8:23 a.m., he regretted the goodwill decision.

His Fiat convertible wouldn't start. He'd parked it in the garage with the lights on when he'd returned home from Ollie's Pub in Enid last night. Jarrod ripped his keys out of the ignition and sat in the car for a moment. The headache that had threatened to claim him since opening his eyes was looming large and close, ready to swallow his thoughts. He got out of the car, went through the house, locked his front door and walked the mile to his downtown office.

The lights were on—the fluorescence hurt his eyes. He smelled Katie's Avon "Candid" perfume and realized he'd forgotten both deodorant and cologne after his shower. He looked around the waiting room and found his patient, Mr. Robert Tate, sitting in a plastic chair, filling out the New Patient paperwork with one hand while holding the left side of his jaw with the other.

Tate looked to be in his late thirties or early forties. Not too well off, judging by the torn and grass-stained khaki pants and old Black Sabbath concert T-shirt. He wore work boots that had never been polished. Probably worked in an oil patch, Jarrod decided, so maybe he was okay financially, just dirty.

"Hello, Mr. Tate," Jarrod said, smiling his friendly dentist smile.

The patient glanced up and groaned a greeting.

"I understand you broke a tooth on a steak bone," Jarrod said. "That's gotta hurt. I'll go get ready. When you're done, Miss Hubbard will bring you back."

The patient groaned again and Jarrod hurried to his first examination room—a square area with heavy crimson drapes for three walls. The wall of the building was the fourth wall; a counter with a sink and some cabinets were mounted on the solid wall. He turned on the faucet over the sink and splashed several handfuls of cold water on his face, just to wash the last of the grogginess from his eyes.

As he dried, Jarrod glanced toward the reception area and saw that Katie Hubbard, his dental hygienist/secretary/sometimes lover was wearing a plain pink T-shirt, high, tight denim shorts and flip-flop shoes. Her natural blonde hair was pulled back in a pony tail and held with a pink scrunchy. She must have felt his eyes on her; she turned to wink at him. He smiled back just as the patient wobbled up to the counter, still holding his jaw. Katie glanced over the information the man had provided, then led him to the closest dental chair. Jarrod pulled on a pair of latex gloves, snapping them as he did, and handed Katie a pair that she put on quietly. She kept her eyes and a sly smile on him as she did it.

Robert Tate had not brushed his teeth recently. Jarrod became sickeningly aware of that fact all too quickly. His toast and coffee swirled in his stomach as he leaned close to look into the small mirror he held in Tate's mouth. It smelled as if the steak Tate had been eating had stayed in his mouth long enough to become putrid. Jarrod drew back and sucked in some untainted air.

"Okay, Mr. Tate, it's not broken, but you've got a nasty cavity in an upper molar. When you bit down on that bone you must have stabbed the cavity. Don't worry, though, we can fill it and you'll be just fine."

"Just pull it, Doc," Tate said, his voice strained.

"Oh, now, there's no need for that," Jarrod said. He reached for a mask and hose attached to a tank behind the chair. "We almost never pull teeth anymore."

"Doctor Golding is very good," Katie piped in. "He's going to give you some nitrous oxide gas and it'll relax you so he can work and you won't feel a thing."

"I'll give you a shot of Novocaine to deaden your gums around that tooth, too," Jarrod added. "You just relax." He fitted the gas mask over Tate's face and turned on the nitrous oxide. Tate's eyes were large and round, brown and bloodshot.

"Please, Doctor Golding, just pull it," Tate said, his voice muffled by the mask.

"You don't really want that," Jarrod said. "I know it hurts, and right now all you want is for the pain to stop. I understand you think just ripping it out at the source is the way to go. Trust me, it's not. You need that tooth and I intend to see that you keep it."

Tate was quiet. Jarrod checked the gas and saw he'd had it a little strong. He turned it down. No harm done, and it had calmed the patient quickly, which Jarrod admitted had been necessary. Tate mumbled something. Jarrod leaned closer to the patient's bad-smelling mouth, lifted the mask a bit, and asked him to repeat it.

"Ullllrrrik said…" Tate moaned, his voice wet and slurred. "…silllllver…"

"Something about silver," Jarrod said, meeting Katie's eyes as he lowered the mask again. "He's asleep now. How's he paying for this?"

"Cash. He gave me a hundred already. Said if it cost more he'd pay when you're done. He peeled the hundred-dollar bill from a roll as big as three of my fingers." Katie held up so many of her delicate fingers as a testament to Tate's wealth.

"Fine. Good. Whatever." Jarrod went to the drawer where he kept his tools and removed a small drill.

"What did you do last night?" Katie asked from behind him, putting her hand on his butt and sliding it around to his crotch. She gripped his penis lightly.

"Went to Enid. Had a few drinks. Thought about you."

"Yeah, but you didn't offer to take me along."

"It was just guy stuff. A bunch of boy dentists watching baseball and getting drunk. That guy's breath is horrible." He motioned at Tate with his head.

"You sure he's out?"

"He better be," Jarrod said. "I doubt he'd like to know he's paying the bill for you to stand here and hold my dick when you could be giving him a shot of Novocaine."

"Fine. Somebody's got a hangover." Katie let him go and went back to the patient. "He really is out. Stone cold. Dear God! His mouth *reeks*."

"Told you."

A few moments later Katie said, "He's still out cold and his gum should be numb."

Jarrod came back to the patient, giving his assistant a small pat on the butt and a wink. Katie smiled, the reprimand she'd received moments ago likely already forgotten. *Big boobs, little brain. Gotta love her.*

"Hold his jaw open." Jarrod took a deep breath and leaned over Tate's face. He squeezed the trigger and the drill in his hand buzzed to life. "I wish he was awake enough to open his mouth. Can you hold it open a little more?"

"Eww. I'd rather hold open a skunk's butt," Katie said, but she spread Tate's jaws further.

The drill hummed and vibrated as Jarrod finished the prep work. Within a minute or so, he had all the infected and decayed bits out of the cavity.

"Suction that out for me, will you?" Jarrod backed away from the patient. He took another deep draught of air, wanting to inhale something that didn't hold the scent of Tate's breath.

As Katie sucked the bits of decay and powdered tooth from Tate's mouth with a small vacuum, Jarrod removed a plastic capsule of amalgam from another cabinet. He bounced it in his rubber-gloved palm. "You asked for silver, you got it," he said. "Sixty-five percent silver in this baby."

Jarrod put the capsule in his triturator and turned it on. The machine shook the capsule vigorously for about six seconds, mixing mercury with the silver, tin, copper and other metals of the alloy tooth filler. Jarrod took the capsule out of the triturator and returned to his patient.

"We are giving him a toothbrush before he leaves, right?" Katie asked.

"I'll give him a dozen," Jarrod answered.

He opened the capsule and Katie bravely opened Tate's mouth again. Jarrod took his amalgam carrier from a tray of instruments and began transferring small amounts of the alloy into the reeking hole of Tate's mouth. Jarrod grinned as he noticed how steady his hands were. No trace of a hangover while he worked. *It's good to be young.*

"Can you hand me the condenser and my mirror?"

Katie reached over Tate's head and retrieved the instruments. "Wouldn't it have been better to use the composite for filling?" she asked. "I mean, the silver never looks very good."

Jarrod took the condenser and gently packed the amalgam into Tate's cavity, watching his movements in the small round mirror on the end of another long steel rod. "The man said silver."

"I hope he didn't mean he didn't want silver," Katie said.

"This molar's far enough back no one's going to see it without crawling into his mouth," Jarrod answered, his voice shorter than he meant. He forced himself to sound nice. "God knows, with breath like this, no one's going to do that."

"That's for sure," Katie said.

"This is really a pretty bad one," he said. "Bad shape. I'm not looking forward to burnishing it.

"How 'bout if I take you to Molly's for lunch when we're finished here? Then we can drive over to Enid for a matinee, mess around, have a nice dinner and come back. Maybe you could stay over tonight."

"Maybe," Katie said. Jarrod heard her smile and knew it would be a lucky night for him. Those long bare legs of Katie's could hold him tighter and squeeze him emptier than any woman he knew.

He was still packing amalgam and thinking of the pleasure he'd have atop his assistant when Tate began to convulse. The man's body jerked wildly and without warning. Jarrod was so startled he dropped his mirror into Tate's mouth. His hand shot forward and grabbed the handle of the tool. Tate's jaws clamped shut, tearing through the thin layer of latex glove and ripping into Jarrod's thumb and forefinger.

"Dear God, get him off!" Jarrod shrieked. "Get him off! Make him let go!"

"Calm down, Jarrod, stop pulling. You're bleeding. It's bad. Stop!" Katie was struggling to pry open the patient's jaws.

Jarrod saw blood—his blood—staining the whites of Tate's teeth. Then he saw that Tate's eyes were open—wide open—and glaring at him. "Let me go, you psycho son of a bitch!" Jarrod screamed.

Something reached up and grabbed Jarrod's shirt. It should have been Tate's hand. But the thing that held him was covered in gray and black hair. Jarrod stared at the limb and watched it lose all human proportions. It was the forearm of an animal, something like a huge dog. He looked back at Tate's face.

The man's features seemed to swell and suddenly pop out of human form. Jarrod stared into the savage eyes of mammoth wolf. With an almost casual flick of its head, the animal got a better grip on the dentist's hand and sank more teeth into it. Jarrod screamed again.

The transformation of the beast was not completed. Or rather, Jarrod saw that the animal was still having convulsions. The hind legs were kicking and scrabbling at the exam chair, shredding the imitation leather of the seat. The boots and pants Tate was wearing had slipped or been torn off and lay on the floor.

Katie had backed away from the struggle. Jarrod looked to her for help just as she became entangled in the drape separating them from the next examination room. She fell backwards and pulled the drape off its rod. She screamed as it fell over her, covering her like a blood-soaked shroud.

Suddenly, the clamp on his arm released. Jarrod looked back to the thing in his chair as he pulled his bleeding hand close to his chest. Tate was in the chair again, slumped sideways, blood and drool running from his perfectly human mouth. Short, thin hairs—wolf hairs—were drifting from his body to the floor. His chest was not moving. Jarrod could hear no breathing.

"Is he dead?" Katie had returned to his side.

"I think so. Check his pulse."

She hesitated, then took a limp wrist between her fingers, keeping her body as far away from the chair as she could. After a moment she put it back in the man's lap.

"He's dead."

"A wolf." Jarrod said the word, then looked at his bloody hand. The wound burned and itched. He looked back to Katie, as if she could offer some logic concerning what had just happened. "He was a... a werewolf."

# KISS OF THE WOLF

Tami broke away from the group of women who had come to the party without men. Their talk was beginning to stray toward the subjects of vibrators and lesbianism. Tami didn't want a machine or another woman, she wanted a man.

She wanted *that* man—the tall one with the long hair and dark suit who had been stealing lingering glances at her all night but had not spoken to her. He had a habit of stroking his crimson necktie. Tami had heard him talking to other guests. His deep voice with its European accent was smooth and incredibly sexy.

Tami went to the punch bowl and was scooping out a helping of the glistening red liquid when she felt someone touch her arm. She looked around and found herself trapped in the deep brown eyes of the stranger.

He took her by the hand and gently led her out of the main room, away from the partiers and their mindless talk. He led her down a long hallway and into a small, dim bedroom. He closed the door and suddenly they were alone. Tami let him lead her to a dressing table and lean her against it.

"You're beautiful," he whispered.

"I didn't get your name," Tami said, her own voice a hoarse whisper. She felt a little silly and slutty, but found the man's actions extremely exciting. He didn't answer her inquiry.

He found her other hand and his fingers caressed up her bare arms to her shoulders, to her neck. He leaned in and kissed her firmly but gently on the mouth. Tami felt her lips parting for his tongue almost as if she had lost control of her will under his touch.

The kiss broke apart slowly. Tami sighed, opened her eyes and found him still staring into them. She tried to kiss him again, but he allowed only a short peck. He smiled quickly, then knelt before her.

His hands rested on her ankles for a moment, then he raised each foot carefully and slipped her shoes off. Again, his hands gently gripped her ankles. Slowly, his fingers began a light, fluttery journey up the sides of her calves, moving inward so that as they passed her knees they continued around to tickle up the back of her thighs. Tami felt goose bumps break out over her body. She became suddenly aware of her nipples standing erect, pressing sensuously against the black satin of her dress.

His hands glided over her silk underwear up to the waistband. Tami stared at the bedroom door, wondering if she should stop him, not wanting to, not sure she could. She glanced down quickly and saw that he was still looking up at her face. He smiled again as his hands began sliding back down her legs, taking her panties with them.

His fingers were like razors of pleasure as they pulled the cotton back over her thighs. At her knees the panties fell away from her legs and he released them. She felt them as they came to rest lightly around her ankles. She started to step out of them, but his next movement stopped her.

His hands raced back up her thighs to the hem of her dress. He pushed the satin slowly up until the hem was at her waist. He was still looking at her face, still smiling just a bit.

"Oh dear God," Tami moaned.

He moved his face forward, his eyes remaining locked with hers until the swell of her breasts hid him from her sight. She knew where he was, though. Her pubic hair was suddenly as sensitive as a cat's whiskers. She felt his lips lightly brush a few strands and it was as if she had been shocked. Then he moved past the barrier of light hair and touched the lips of her vagina gently with his mouth. He kissed her, teasing her. Tami felt as if she would melt and slide into his mouth and down his throat and live forever inside him.

But it was he who entered her. His lips parted hers and his tongue, the same burning tongue that had been in her mouth only moments before, found her clitoris. Tami gasped as he stroked her moist insides firmly a few times. Soon, his tongue was moving more quickly, flicking around within her like a candle flame in a stiff breeze, then pressing and rolling hot against her clitoris.

Tami sucked in her breath. She wished she could whisper the man's name over and over as he pushed her up the slope toward the pinnacle of ecstasy. She leaned back and reached behind her to balance herself against the dressing table. She realized her hips were rocking gently and she felt as though every organ in her body had lost its moorings and was oozing toward his dancing tongue.

Her nipples burned. She raised a hand and touched one through the satin of her dress. She squeezed it, then cupped the entire breast and squeezed that. She trusted more of her balance to the dressing table and to his face and brought her other hand slowly up the slick fabric of her dress to cradle her other breast. Then both hands slid down, down over the satin and through the soft patch of her pubic hair until her hands were holding his head as it moved back and forth, back and forth, his tongue going incredibly deep inside her.

Tami moaned and gave herself totally to the moment. She raised her right leg, her cotton panties slipped from her ankle like a broken shackle and she hooked her leg over his back as her fingers locked in his hair. With her leg and her hands she pressed him forward, burying him in her, pinning his face against her swollen, secret part, drowning him in the juice of her need. Still his tongue danced, deeper inside her now, hotter because of the heat surrounding it.

Hooks pierced her flesh and began to pull slowly, slowly... and then abruptly ripped her apart as an orgasm like a crashing meteorite tore through her from her groin up to the tips of her hair and down to her curling toes. Tami heard a scream and knew it was her own and she didn't care. She hoped everyone in the house heard her and tore down the bedroom door and saw her as she died on this stranger's face.

He didn't relent as the first orgasm ebbed, but continued to lick and suck desperately as one after another the waves of pleasure pounded through her and flowed over him. Tami gasped and moaned and fought to remain standing as the strong hand of ecstasy gripped her and squeezed over and over, leaving her weaker each time. She sagged against the table, her fingers still locked in his hair.

His hair... there was too much of it. And something was in it... something velvety but stiff.

Tami looked down as her last orgasm came, a small but draining outpouring that ended in another scream, but this scream was a sound of terror.

The thing crouching between her legs was no longer a man. He still wore the dark suit and blood-red tie of the man who had brought her to the room, but now he had the head and face of a beast.

*Of a wolf.*

Tami could see her own moisture glistening in the black and gray hair of the beast's face. The animal's eyes looked up at her, its snout still buried between her legs. Then she felt the teeth, felt her flesh tear and the hot blood begin to flow. She screamed again and tried to scramble away, but the wolf-man had her crotch clamped in the vice of his jaws.

The door of the room opened and another man entered. He was an older man, very thick and solid looking, with a thick beard. He was very naked. His clothes were rolled into a bundle he carried under his right arm.

"Help me," Tami begged, one hand stretched toward the naked man.

"Luther McGrath, turn around," the naked man commanded in a rich voice that reverberated through the bedroom. He tossed his clothes aside and locked the door behind him.

The teeth released her and Tami fell off the dressing table. The pain seemed to be even worse now that the fangs were removed from her flesh. She put a hand between her legs and it came away glistening a bright red. Blood raced down her wrist toward her elbow.

The wolf-man rose to his feet with the grace of an animal, his features melting back to those of a man. A shower of fine wolf hairs floated down and stuck to the blood on Tami's hand.

"Ulrik," the wolf-man growled. "The man who would be father of the Pack. I've heard how you look for the woman who will be the Mother. You're a fool. You are not the one who will find her."

"The Mother has been found," Ulrik said. "Our messiah has been born already. The Pack is gathering, Luther McGrath. There can be no culls among us.

84

"You are a danger to the Pack," he said. He waved a hand toward Tami. "Look at what you have done. What will you do with her? Would you leave her so that someone else finds her and thinks she has been mauled by a dog? In this room, in this house, with several dozen guests downstairs? You will expose us before we are ready."

"You forget that not everyone agrees with you on the issue of your harlot and her son," Luther said. "The Pack will gather, yes, but when we do, we will not follow your bitch's half-breed. It will be a son born to me."

The man called Luther charged across the room toward the other man. Tami screamed again as Luther's shape changed from man to full-fledged wolf. The naked man, Ulrik, transformed his shape in the time it took for Tami to draw a new breath. Ulrik raced to meet Luther's charge.

The wolf who was Luther became tangled in his clothes. Ulrik caught him, bowled him over, his jaws locking with a snap on Luther's throat. Tami groaned as Ulrik tugged at the other wolf. Luther thrashed and snapped and growled. Saliva and blood spattered across the room in a thick spray. Ulrik's mouth tore free. A gout of blood erupted from Luther's throat. Ulrik did not stop. He pounced on the body, grabbed the ruined neck between his teeth and planted his forepaws on the dying wolf's shoulder. He pulled.

Luther's head made a tearing, snapping, wet sound as it separated from his body. Ulrik opened his jaws and dropped the head.

Tami's vision was turning black around the edges. She could no longer feel the blood running from the wound between her legs. She didn't think she could have lost enough blood to be dying, although she was lying in a large, wet puddle on the carpet. She blinked, trying to push herself to her elbows. When she opened her eyes, Ulrik was crouching before her. He had returned to his human shape but was still naked.

"I am sorry such a thing has happened to you," he said, his voice gentle and filled with concern. He helped her to a sitting position leaning against the dressing table. "However, what is done is done. You must make a decision now."

Tami could only blink at him again.

"You can become one of us," Ulrik said.

Tami looked past Ulrik to the body of the man-beast who had given her oral sex and inflicted the damning wound on her. She looked back to Ulrik.

"A werewolf?"

He nodded.

Tami closed her eyes and shook her head. "No."

"So be it, my cub," Ulrik said. "The Gift is not meant for everyone."

Tami felt his strong, hard hands cradle her face. His grasp tightened just a bit; he deftly twisted her neck to the right and she knew no more.

# To be a Mother

The woman parked her four-wheel-drive Ford Explorer a block away from the babysitter's house. Two police cars were at the home. She could see one uniformed officer walking along the side of the house, examining it, then he disappeared into the back yard. With a shaking hand, the woman pushed a lock of her raven-black hair behind her ear. She dug her cell phone from her purse and turned it on; she had several messages. She dialed the number to play them. As she listened, a finger pushed past her lips and pressed against the sharp edge of a broken tooth.

Ellie Sutter's frantic voice screeched from the little phone. "Lana, where are you? Oh, it's horrible. He's gone. Danny's gone. Call me!" A second message from the babysitter repeated the same general information and added that she was calling the police. A third simply said, "Where are you!" The fourth message was from a cop.

"Miss Redleaf, this is Detective Darrell Johnston of the Amarillo Police Department," said the deep male voice. "I'm calling because your child care provider, Miss Ellen Sutter, has reported your son missing from her facility. Please call me back immediately." He left a number.

The woman who called herself Lana Redleaf dropped the cell phone back into her purse. Her hands shook. She saw that one wrist still had wisps of short black hairs, like dog hairs, clinging to it. She brushed them off and turned her attention back to the police cars.

"Oh Danny," she moaned. "My baby. My baby. I never should have left you." There had been no other option, though. She knew that. She couldn't take the toddler into the field with her. She started her SUV, backed around the nearest corner, then raced for home.

She parked her Explorer in a shopping center parking lot a half-mile from her rental house, tucked her long hair into her sweat suit jacket and pulled the hood up. She put on sunglasses, then left the vehicle.

"You bastard," she muttered as she walked toward home. "I know you're behind this, Ulrik. You just can't stand that I have a son."

From two blocks away she didn't notice anything unusual in the neighborhood—no unfamiliar vans or strangers loitering near-by. Still, she went around to the alley and hurried through her back gate, the surrounding dogs setting up their usual racket as she did so, making her think it would have been less conspicuous to use the front door, after all. She unlocked her back door and slipped inside.

The two-bedroom house was dark. The shades and curtains were drawn, blocking out the small amount of sunlight filtering through the overcast day in the Texas panhandle. The woman moved quickly through the utility room and kitchen to the living room. Photographs of Danny playing in a nearby park, of him eating chocolate cake, digging in the mud and doing other things little boys did filled frames hung over the sofa. A 10-by-13-inch portrait of the toddler hung over the entertainment center, his chubby cheeks puffed out in a big smile that showed two rows of shiny white baby teeth. He was wearing a navy blue sailor suit. His blond hair curled around his ears and one pudgy hand was raised in a half-wave.

"Damn you, Ulrik. Why couldn't you just leave us alone?"

She was reaching for the frame, to remove the portrait so she could take it with her, when the front door was shaken by heavy knocks. The woman looked toward the door and saw that the only uncovered window in the house was the small diamond in the front door. A man's face peered through the window. His eyes locked with hers. She dropped her hands and went to the door.

"Ma'am, I'm Detective Johnston, Amarillo police," the man said, holding a badge in front of him for a moment. "You're Lana Redleaf?" The man's face was lined, his hair mussed and his brown suit jacket had a well-worn look. His necktie was a slightly lighter shade of brown, with subtle yellow circular designs. He did not smile or nod at her. His eyes fixed on her face and never wavered.

The woman's voice caught in her throat for a moment and she was unable to answer. She nodded.

"You've heard that your son is missing?" the man asked.

"Yes," the woman said. "I came to get his picture. For identification. To make posters."

"Why didn't you return my call?" he asked. "May I come in?"

"Oh. Yes. Please." The woman stepped aside, then closed the door once the man was in her house. He glanced at a light switch and she reluctantly turned on the overhead lamps.

"Why didn't you call?"

"I don't know. I just felt... numb. I had messages from Ellie, too. I just... I don't know."

"Ma'am, do you have the birth certificate for your son? Something with fingerprints or footprints?"

"No—no, I don't. I gave birth at home. With a midwife."

"There still should be a record," he said. "Tell me again where you've been for the past week."

"Out. In the grasslands. I'm studying the wildlife there."

"Miss Sutter says you go out there for a week every month. Is that correct?"

"Usually. Yes. I'm working on an important project for the university."

The detective chewed his lip for a moment, as if thinking about something very difficult. Finally he unbuttoned his shirt pocket and pulled out a folded piece of paper. He unfolded it and held it toward the woman, his eyes on her face the entire time. "Is this your son?"

The woman looked at the paper, which contained a black-and-white image of the boy she called Danny as he had looked eight months earlier. The word "Missing" was printed in bold block letters above the photo. Beneath the picture, the child was identified as Dean Osborne, age nine months, reported missing from a county fair in Newkirk, Oklahoma.

"No. No, that's not my son," the woman said.

"I see." The detective let his bright blue eyes slide away from her face to the gallery of photos hanging on the wall over the couch. "I can't help but notice the child in your photos here looks an awful lot like the boy in this picture. These where he's younger—" He raised a finger to point toward the picture of Danny eating cake.

"No! I told you already."

"I also notice that your son has a very fair complexion, and yet you appear to be a full-blooded American Indian. Sioux, if I remember the tribal roll correctly."

"His father is white. Very fair complected," the woman answered.

"Ma'am, I'm afraid I'm going to have to take you to the station to answer some questions," the detective said. "From what your babysitter has told us and from the pictures you have here, we have reason to believe the child you claim is your son is the boy in this photograph." He waved the printed paper at her as he folded it to return it to his pocket.

"I can't go," the woman said. "My baby is missing. I have to find my baby. Why aren't you looking for my—" Before she could finish, her cell phone started ringing. She and the cop looked toward her purse.

"Let me get that," he said.

"No, you have no right to…"

The man picked up her purse, unzipped it and pulled out the phone. He pushed a button and put it to his ear. "Hello," he said, then paused. "Yes, she's here. This is Detective Darrell Johnston of the Amarillo police. May I ask who's calling?" Another pause. "Just a moment." He held the phone toward the woman. She took it and stepped away from the policeman.

"Hello?" she said.

"Kiona Brokentooth. How many times must we do this?" a man's voice asked.

"You..." she began, then stopped herself, glancing at the detective from the corner of her eye. "Why do you do this?"

"You have company, Kiona."

"Yes."

"I am sorry that it must involve the police this time. That was not my intention. You must face the truth, my cub. You are not to be the Mother. You cannot bear children. You cannot fool us, either."

"That isn't true," Kiona said. "No other woman is like me. You have never heard of another who had the dreams I had, who could run with the wolves even before you gave me the Gift. I am—"

"You are not destined to be Mother of the Pack, Kiona," the man said. "The child must be returned."

"Ulrik, you bastard. I want him back. Bring him back! Bring him—"

"Give me the phone!" Detective Darrell Johnston was suddenly at her side, his hand struggling to pull the phone away from the woman's ear. "Give me that phone," he shouted again.

Kiona Brokentooth shoved the detective away from her, letting the phone fall to the floor. The cop tripped on a leg of the coffee table and stumbled, crashing to the floor. A hand reached toward the gun he carried under his jacket, then stopped. His eyes widened. His mouth opened and worked uselessly. A stain spread across his lap.

Kiona let out a roar as she dropped to all fours. As she moved, her shape seemed to melt like a wax figurine left too close to a flame. Before she was on the floor, the metamorphosis was complete. As a black wolf, she stood before the detective, her lips pulled back to show her savage teeth, including an incisor that had been broken before she had learned to change her shape. The green sweat suit jacket hung loosely on her upper body; the pants had fallen away during the change. Kiona studied the detective for a moment, enjoying his fear.

She lunged at Johnston, pinned him to the floor and ripped out his throat. The taste of blood excited her fury, drowning her loss for the moment, and she tore madly at the bleeding body, not stopping until the face was unrecognizable, the jacket, shirt and flesh torn to shreds over his chest. She heard her name being called and backed away from the body.

"Kiona!" The voice was coming from the cellular telephone. The wolf melted and transformed into the woman again. She stood up, brushing loose wolf hairs from her legs as she did so. She could feel the hairs trapped inside her jacket. Blood dripped from her mouth and chin, but she ignored it. She picked up the phone.

"Ulrik. I want him back."

"You made sure the policeman is dead?" Josef Ulrik asked.

"He's dead. I want Danny back."

"He is not your son. I am taking him back to his rightful parents."

"You can't do that to me!" Kiona screamed. "Fine! I'm not your chosen one. I'm not the one werewolf who can give birth naturally. I've accepted that. But I want a baby. Damn you, Ulrik, I want a baby."

"Please do not cry, Kiona," Ulrik urged. "It is not meant to be."

"It isn't fair."

"Life seldom is fair."

"Tell me the secret to giving the Gift to a baby. Your maker did it to you when you were a baby. You must know how."

"I will not tell you." Ulrik's voice was firm. "It is not wise to do so. You have learned not to attempt it without the elixir. You will not try that again."

"No. Never. Never again." Kiona closed her eyes but could not block out the picture of another child, an infant boy, struggling to change shape a month after she had bitten him. "No," she repeated as the image in her mind once again broke apart into a half-dozen ragged, writhing pieces of bloody, hairy flesh. She remembered afterward, when she had admitted what she'd done, Ulrik told her that a child so young must be eased through the process with an ancient serum. *How can he deny me the formula?*

"This is for the best, Kiona," Ulrik said. "Trust me."

She couldn't reply.

92

"You must leave there now. You will be all right?"

"I'll be fine."

"Kiona? Must I again come and rescue another stolen baby from you in a few years' time?"

"You could leave me alone."

"I cannot do that. I cannot allow you to draw such attention to the Pack."

"I just want a baby of my own," Kiona said. "I can't adopt. You know that, not with my aliases and fake ID's, no job, mysterious disappearances every month where I can't take a baby who can't change shape with me."

"After I return him, I will remain in the area to protect this child from you until I deem it safe," Ulrik said. "I suggest you go into hiding for a while. Good-bye, Kiona. Good-bye, my cub."

The phone beeped and was dead in her hand.

Kiona returned the phone to her purse, put on her pants, and went to her bedroom. She threw clothes, cash and false identification papers into a suitcase. She put the suitcase, her purse and the framed portrait of "Danny" by her front door. She went to the bathroom and washed the blood from her face and hair, then hurried out the front door and back to the shopping center for her Explorer. She roared back to her driveway, left the engine running while she loaded her things, then hurried out of town.

In Santa Fe, New Mexico, she sat in her SUV and watched an Hispanic man and woman playing with five children in a park near a small lake. As the parents turned all their attention to congratulating the oldest girl on the fish she pulled from the water, Kiona slipped from her vehicle. Quickly and silently, she approached the picnic table where a baby boy was cooing in an infant seat.

The idea had come to her as she crossed the border from Texas into New Mexico. Ulrik said he would be guarding Danny to keep her from returning and trying to reclaim him. That would keep him in Oklahoma, at least for a while. *That should give me some time.*

She snatched the infant carrier from the picnic table and ran.

By the time the baby's mother turned back to the table there was no sign of the kidnapper other than a flash of brake lights as the Ford left the park and headed for the mountains.

# About the Author

Steven E. Wedel is a life-long Oklahoman who grew up in Enid and currently lives in Moore with his wife and four children. He is an award-winning journalist and fiction author who has worked for The Daily Oklahoman, The Journal Record and numerous other newspapers. His other books include *Darkscapes, Murdered by Human Wolves, Shara,* and *Seven Days in Benevolence.*

Wedel holds a bachelor's degree in journalism and a master's degree in liberal studies, creative writing emphasis. You can visit him online at www.stevenewedel.com.

Don't miss the first book of Steven E. Wedel's *Werewolf Saga:*

> *Murdered By Human Wolves*

Based on a true story, *Murdered By Human Wolves* tells the tale of Kathering Cross, a young woman who was killed in 1917. Her tombstone in Konawa, OK bears the epitaph "Murdered By Human Wolves"

Visit www.scrybepress.com for details or call 1-866-343-4516 to order direct from the publisher.

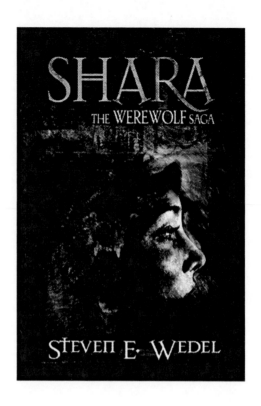

BOOK *l* OF THE *WEREWOLF SAGA: SHARA*

SHARA ONLY WANTS TO LIVE A NORMAL, HAPPY LIFE WITH HER NEW HUSBAND AND THEIR INFANT SON. BUT THE PACK HAS FOUND HER...

SHE IS THE ONE, THE MOTHER, THE ONLY WERE-WOLF WHO CAN BEAR LIVE CHILDREN FOR THE PACK...

Printed in the United States
79889LV00001B/178-183

9 781933 274058